An Unnecessary Diversion

Flora Vincent-James

Copyright © 2020 Flora Vincent-James

All rights reserved, including the right to reproduce this book, or portions thereof in any form. No part of this text may be reproduced, transmitted, downloaded, decompiled, reverse engineered, or stored, in any form or introduced into any information storage and retrieval system, in any form or by any means, whether electronic or mechanical without the express written permission of the author.

This is a work of fiction. Names and characters are the product of the author's imagination and any resemblance to actual persons, living or dead, is entirely coincidental.

The views expressed in this work are solely those of the author and do not necessarily reflect the views of the publisher, and the publisher hereby disclaims any responsibility for them.

ISBN: 9798645600662

PublishNation
www.publishnation.co.uk

For my family, especially my sister, who has given me more inspiration and encouragement than she will ever know.

1

If he had been interested in the confusing complexities of matters of human emotion, rather than the recently discarded remains of a bag of chips on the sea wall, a seagull, perched high on the top of an ornate cast iron Victorian lamppost, would have detected an aura of acute sadness circulating around the wooden bench below him. Similarly, a small dog, straining hard on a lead held by his elderly, watery-eyed owner, was oblivious to the sombre mood of a melancholy couple as he hurried by that same wooden bench. His nose was scanning the ground; he was entirely focused on the varied and interesting odours of the wide concrete promenade.

 The grey English Channel was chopping its way into the pebbly beach as the incoming tide pushed forward. Salt spray was carried in the cold late afternoon breeze across the sea wall to the bench and the ribbon of municipal garden beyond. The breeze was serenading the beach and the buildings dotted along the promenade; a mournful song, performed in a minor key with percussion accompaniment courtesy of a metal flagpole and its line. Behind the garden was a road and on the other side of that was a long terrace of grand, white painted, five storey houses and hotels, some with turrets adorning the roofline. Anyone standing at the window of one of those hotel rooms now could have looked across the road, garden and promenade to the sea and seen the pier jutting out into the water, its iron stilts rusty but resolutely defying the onslaught of the brisk advancing tide. They might have noticed the seagull swooping down from the lamppost to the bag of chips or the little dog, scurrying along and his owner with outstretched arm tottering along behind. They might also have seen the couple on the bench, eye to eye, and engaged in earnest conversation. The man was gently stroking his companion's cheek with the backs of his fingers and the wind was whipping her blonde hair out behind her.

By the time the seagull had reached its starchy supper and begun to peck enthusiastically inside the greasy paper with its sharp yellow beak, the dog's owner had been dragged along several yards towards a hexagonal kiosk where the tired owner was now fastening the shutters. Business had been quiet today; cold wind and grey skies were not conducive to good sales of refreshments, buckets and spades or postcards. After locking the final shutter, the owner dropped his keys into the inside pocket of his overcoat and made his way along the promenade towards the bus stop. He would only need to travel three stops to his home. His wife would be already there, standing at the kitchen stove stirring a saucepan full of something warming and delicious. He was so engrossed with the thought of domestic comfort that he was barely aware of the little dog scuttling by or the cacophony of seagull calls as several of them amassed on the sea wall in close proximity to the chips and the original bird that had sparked their interest.

The driver of bus number 36 which, in a few minutes, would collect the kiosk owner and transport him to a stop on the western end of his circular route, was now turning his busy vehicle out of a side road onto the main seafront and beginning his steady progress towards the pier. The tall white buildings were on his right hand side and the long strip of well-tended gardens with adjacent promenade was on his left. The driver's next stop would be the pier entrance and he could see a solitary woman waiting there with left arm raised to indicate her intention to board. She had a headscarf tied tightly under her chin and held a wicker shopping basket in the crook of her other arm. The bus pulled over and the woman got on. She made her way along the row of seats and sat down in a vacant one on the promenade side, pulling the wicker basket on to her lap so that there would be space for someone to sit next to her. The bus set off again and the woman looked out of the window at the dark agitated sea and the horizon which blurred into a monotonous and colourless sky above. She was thinking of her beloved elderly parents and the day she had just spent in their company, happily cleaning and cooking for them. In her wicker basket were the ingredients for the next meal she would have to prepare when she got home to her family. The bus slowly picked up speed and halfway along the seafront road she witnessed an altercation between several seagulls on the sea wall.

Just beyond was a bench, where two people were sitting. The man had his arm around the woman and she was resting her head on his shoulder. His head was bent down towards her and although his face was partially obscured, the woman on the bus could sense that this was not a happy conversation. A little further on and the bus passed an elderly gentleman, stooped with age and walking quicker than he probably would have liked due to his energetic canine companion. The bus bell rang and the lumbering vehicle pulled in at the next stop. Three passengers alighted and several more boarded, the kiosk owner being one of them. He sat down next to a woman with a wicker basket on her lap.

The bus rumbled on until it came to the end of the seafront, then turned right and travelled along a narrower road with Victorian terraced houses on each side. The kiosk owner observed their familiar features; bay windows downstairs, mostly with net curtains obscuring the interiors and tiny front gardens with tiled paths running up from the gate to the front doors. Some houses had been rendered and painted in white or pastel shades, whilst others still displayed the original red brick. Chimneys were dotted along the roofline and many of them were emitting curling smoke which was absorbed quickly by the cool late afternoon air. At the first two stops along this long straight road the kiosk owner would avert his gaze from the houses and absentmindedly watch the movements of various passengers getting off and on the bus, and while the bus was stopped outside the Wagon and Horses, he caught the strains of 'Old Man' drifting from a partially open window on the first floor of the pub. Some of the notes were being consumed by the distance and the salty breeze, but the melody and the lyrics were still easily identifiable and, although exquisitely and gently crafted by Mr Young, they punched their way into the kiosk owner's chest and rose up into his throat. The bus moved on and at the third stop it was his turn to get off. He rose from his seat and made his way to the exit, politely smiling at a tall man who was about to board the bus but stood back allow him to step down from the bus first. The tall man had to bend his head as he walked down the bus between the row of seats until he found an empty one. On the opposite side of the aisle he noticed a woman wearing a headscarf. An elderly woman had just sat down on the seat in front of him. She was wearing a thick wool coat and tiny droplets of diamond drizzle were sparkling on the damp fabric which was emitting a slightly musty, but not necessarily unpleasant, aroma. The mustiness wormed its way into the subconscious of the tall man who found himself briefly recollecting his late grandmother standing in front of her Victorian fireplace; looking in the mirror above it and adjusting her coat and velvet hat, complete with hat pin, in preparation for her walk to church. The bus driver pulled away again and number 36 lumped and clanked along for a few hundred yards. The driver focused his attention on the end of the street where he would have to slow down to a stop and carefully position his vehicle at the junction with the next street. He was now at the far end of his route and would begin the journey back in an easterly direction. He checked for traffic and made his right turn manoeuvre with customary precision. The next stop, in about four hundred yards, would be the Post Office, which by now would be closed for the day. Next to the Post Office was a sweet shop, displaying an impressive array of large, brightly coloured screw top sweet jars in the window. Pear drops, lemon bonbons, chocolate limes, fruit salads, aniseed balls, mint humbugs, jelly beans and barley sugars adorned the top window shelf, the remaining shelves containing similar colourful sugary confection. The woman with the headscarf stood up ready to get off, placing her wicker basket over her right forearm and steadying herself by hanging on to the back of the seats with her left hand until the bus came to a standstill and she was able to alight. From his seat inside the bus the tall man watched her walking quickly and purposefully along the pavement until the bus was moving again and she was no longer visible. The bus turned once more, back on to the seafront road and this time travelling in the opposite direction. The tall man pulled out a book from his coat pocket and began to read. He didn't see an elderly gentleman unlocking his front door and entering his house with his small dog. Neither did he notice a boarded up kiosk several hundred yards further on, nor an embracing couple, standing in front of a bench. He was reading 'Islands in the Stream' and had already reached, and been moved by, the excruciatingly sad part. After the bus turned off the seafront road, the tall man looked up from his book every now and then, just to check the progress of his homeward journey. He didn't want to miss his stop as dusk was now beginning to fall and he was keen to get home to his young family and the warmth of a coal fire. After several stops, he got off the bus, which was now rounding the top end of the route and about to retrace its westerly path once more.

For the eleventh time that day bus number 36 pulled out on to the road between the tall white buildings and the long strip of gardens. The ornate Victorian lampposts and the windows of the tall buildings were now lighting up, sending out a warm lemon glow into the enveloping darkness. At the pier stop a young woman and her small son, probably aged about seven or eight, got off. The boy took his mother's hand. After making sure they were safely down on the pavement the driver checked his mirrors ready to pull out again. He edged the bus slowly forward and put on his wipers as steady rain had now replaced the squally drizzle and it was beginning to snake across the windscreen. Halfway along the seafront road was a man walking away from a bench, his head down and collar pulled up as defence against the cold sea air and the rain. Without looking the man stepped off the pavement into the path of the bus. The driver hauled on the brakes and the passengers cried out as they were flung forward from their seats. Realising what he had just done, the horrified man in the road with the pulled up collar turned to face the bus, raised his arm to the shocked driver and mouthed 'Sorry. I'm so sorry,' then ran the rest of the way across the road to the safety of the opposite pavement and disappeared from sight. The shaken driver got out of his cab seat and walked round to address his passengers to ensure they were all uninjured. A tin of garden peas which had fallen out of someone's shopping bag, rolled slowly across the bus floor and stopped at the driver's feet. He picked it up and returned it to its owner. Confident that the escaped tinned vegetables were the only casualty of the incident, his fear of mass injury was allayed; he got back into his seat, took a deep breath, and continued his journey.

The young woman with the small boy walked quickly along the promenade in the direction of their home. They passed a woman walking in the opposite direction who had just picked up her handbag from a, now empty, wooden bench.

'Mummy, why is that lady crying?'

2

A large blue removal van pulled into the drive of 186 Winchester Road. The driver carefully negotiated his vehicle into a position which would facilitate easy loading. Long, early morning shadows from the tall conifers on the boundary with the house next door stretched across the driveway and the front of the house, casting mottled darkness on the 1960's render and large picture windows of the ground floor. The rest of the house - the upper half - was caressed by sparkling golden sunshine. A raised flower bed beneath the trees was displaying a mixture of early springtime loveliness; lemon-yellow primroses, daffodils and hyacinths. A blackbird skipped around the flowers and the bare stemmed shrubs, pecking in the damp earth and tossing fallen leaves about to extract its breakfast.

186 Winchester Road had been, until today, owned for three years by Edward and Molly Greenacre. At forty seven years of age, Edward, once again, felt the need to move on and thus try and satisfy the restlessness which had been a part of his life since he was a child. He had been born in 1926, the year of the General Strike. The young Edward had been brought up in a home with doting parents who lavished copious amounts of love and affection upon him but, nevertheless he had suffered a childhood which had been punctuated by trauma. Severe ill health, family tragedy and war had a profound and lasting effect on him.

None of the troubles of his early life were affecting Edward today, however. Optimism was surging through his circulatory system. He was a qualified architect. He was in his prime. He was magnificent and invincible. This was 1973 and he was going to set alight the Planning Department of the Council in South Humberside where he was about to take up a new a job. He would be generously imparting all the knowledge he had acquired over the last twenty five years to his new colleagues. He was going to command the respect he deserved. The contents of 186 Winchester Road had been packed up into tea chests ready for this new and rewarding phase of his life, and the previous three years of disappointment could be drop kicked with huge enthusiasm over the southern counties horizon.

Edward was a tall lean man, classically handsome with his pale blue-grey eyes and dark thick wavy hair, showing only a few flecks of silver at his temples. He always dressed well, rarely leaving the house without a clean perfectly ironed shirt and silk tie. Even today, moving day, was no exception. He had on a navy blue suit, white shirt and light blue tie. The ensemble was finished with a silk handkerchief which had been neatly folded into the breast pocket of his jacket.

'Molly. Van's here.' To make this announcement Edward had walked into the kitchen where his wife was preparing a pot of tea for the removal men. Edward was not one for calling from another room or raising his voice in any way. Gentle was his byword.

'Right. Well, I'm nearly ready. Just got these last few things to put in that box.' Molly gestured towards a collection of cups and plates which had been used for breakfast but were now washed up and ready to wrap in some old newspapers which had been given to her by their elderly next door neighbour.

'I'll come back and do that after I've let the men in if you like. Give you a chance to get upstairs and finish emptying the last few bits and pieces from the cupboards,' said Edward.

Molly put the tea cosy over the teapot and made her way upstairs to pack the last few remaining items in the bedrooms.

Edward walked back to the front of the house and opened the door.

'Good morning. Do come in,' said Edward. 'We're all set. Where would you like to start? Downstairs or up?'

He extended his hand towards the van driver who shook it warmly and declared that he and his colleague would start with the large items of furniture in the living room.

Edward returned to the kitchen and picked up a newspaper ready to start wrapping. He spread out a copy of the Daily Mirror dated the first of January 1973.

'A DAY IN HISTORY' declared the headline in huge black letters across the front page. 'GREAT BRITAIN GOES INTO

GREATER EUROPE'. Edward noted how the words 'Great' and 'Greater' had been underlined, and turned the page over to look at page two. 'Today is the day of the Great Happening,' declared the second page. 'January the first, 1973, begins one of the most significant New Years in the history of our nation. AT LAST the British are members of the European Economic Community, so modestly called the Common Market. This is more than the most elaborate trading agreement in the history of nation states. It is more than the greatest trading bloc in the entire world. It is a community of nations who will grow ever closer as the years pass.'

Further down page two Edward read a sentence which, had the Daily Mirror had any idea who he was, might have written it with him in mind. 'We should, every one of us, be brimful of rejoicing and hope. The spirit of adventure should be coursing in our veins.'

It was a spirit of adventure which was going to take Edward, and his family, two hundred and forty miles northward. Onwards to a better career and better prospects. The Daily Mirror and Edward Greenacre were buoyant and positive, both focusing on a future which they believed promised fulfilment which could not be tarnished.

Edward had taken much pleasure in handing in his notice at the college where he had been lecturing in Building Construction for the last three years. Yes, he would miss teaching and the rapport he was able to build with his students but he certainly would not miss that twit Ferguson, the Head of Department who seemed incapable of making sensible decisions. Edward's view was that a Department Head's role was to run things efficiently for the benefit of the students. They were, after all, at the core of everything they did at the college. However, Edward was not one to feel bitter about what had happened several weeks earlier. He would simply pick himself up, dust himself off and move on. That's what he was doing now and it was going to be Ferguson's loss.

Molly had listened intently to her husband's opinion on the Head's ineptitude and lack of good judgement when he arrived home from college on the final day of the summer term the previous year.

'News of the promotion, Molly. It's not good. They've given it to Phillips and the decision was taken by that idiot, Ferguson. Why on earth would he think that Phillips of all people is worthy of a senior position? The man's not properly qualified, he's lazy, arrogant - just a complete buffoon.'

Edwards's bitter disappointment was obvious.

'And I'll tell you what. This is the worst thing. His attitude towards the students is dreadful. He can't command a class properly and if any of them need extra help he regards it as an inconvenience. I just can't see him being able to handle this promotion. He's not capable. Of course, he's done the rounds of ingratiating himself with those in power, sucking up to Ferguson in particular. I've seen it happen, Molly. It's so obvious. Where's the man's pride, I ask you?'

'Oh dear, Ed. It does seem like a very strange decision, after what you've told me.'

'Indeed. Well, there we are. We can't do anything about it now. The place is corrupt. The powers that be have spoken. And there won't be any more openings coming up anytime soon.'

Two weeks after the unsatisfactory promotion had been announced Edward sat in his little study in 186 Winchester Road with a pile of newspapers and journals stacked on his desk. He was scouring them for job vacancies, boldly circling all those for which he would apply. It wasn't just the failure to secure the Senior Lecturer position which prompted him to look for alternative employment, it was also his inability to settle and his persistent quest for change, although the latter reasons were less obvious to him. He handwrote several letters of application and later Molly would type them up for him on a little manual typewriter, correcting his spelling and grammatical errors and keeping a carbon copy of each which she would file neatly in a cardboard box.

As he wrote, Edward glanced up every now and then to look out of the French windows at the garden. The mid-summer sun was high in the sky and the black shadows were short. He could see his daughters and two of their friends making a den on the lawn, using two wooden linen horses and a collection of old blankets. Over the last couple of years Molly had made an excellent job of improving the garden; hydrangeas, geraniums and phlox held their colourful heads to the light and the lawn was verdant and neatly edged around the borders and the little pond. The girls had spread out a picnic rug in front of their partly constructed den and put down some plates which Molly was going to be filling with cheese, lettuce and salad cream sandwiches later. She had grown the lettuce herself in a little vegetable patch in the far corner of the garden and, following an embarrassing incident two years previously in which a small acid green caterpillar introduced himself from some leaves on a plate which had been presented to Edward's horrified mother, was going to be washed carefully.

After several weeks, and two interviews, one of the applications had come to fruition.

'Edward,' called Molly from the hallway of 186 Winchester Road.

'Post has arrived. There's a letter from the Council in Humberside.'

Edward came downstairs and took the letter from Molly, opening it carefully with a letter opener which they kept in a pot on top of the bureau in the space under the staircase.

'Dear Mr Greenacre,' Edward read aloud.

'Further to your recent application … blah blah blah … and our subsequent meeting on November 3rd 1972, I am pleased to be able to offer you the position of Planning and Contracts Officer. Excellent!' Edward said.

'Great news, Ed. You thought the interview had gone well, didn't you?'

'Yes. I had a good feeling about this one. Right from the start.'

'So you'll accept it then?' asked Molly.

'Of course. There's a huge amount of work the Council will have to get through with this GIA scheme. It will be rather exciting to be there at the outset of the implementation.'

Edward tucked the letter neatly back into its envelope.

'We'll celebrate tonight Molly. I'll pick up a bottle of wine on my way home after work.'

'Well done dear,' replied Molly and kissed her husband on the cheek.

3

So here was a buoyant and quietly excited Edward, four and half months later, standing in the kitchen with just a few items ready to go into a packing box. Edward wrapped the crockery and packed it neatly.

The two employees of Hammonds Removals worked deftly and respectfully, filling the van first with the dark red velour settees, followed by the teak dining table and chairs, the matching sideboard and bookcases and numerous tea chests.

The remaining rooms were also efficiently emptied of their contents and within two hours the house was empty and echoey. Molly walked round the bare rooms for one final clean and check for any forgotten items, feeling sad and devoid of any of the optimism of her husband. However, she assured herself that she was unwaveringly loyal, had been through this process several times already since their marriage in 1952, and would never allow her fears, or even her own desires, to get in the way of support for Edward, whom she loved dearly. Her matrimonial responsibilities were paramount. For better, for worse.

'Ed, dear. I'm all done now. Just going to walk round to Diana's to collect the girls.'

'Right oh. I'll be locking up. Van's just left so I can get the car out of the garage.'

Molly pulled on her coat and shoes and walked the short distance along a footpath to her friend's house. It seemed her life was being divided into chunks, each ragged piece determined by Edward's career requirements and inability to commit to 'something'. Many times over the years Molly had tried to interpret and understand Ed's seemingly constant need for change. Each time they moved on, she had accepted his decision, quietly questioning his reasoning in her mind only and wondering what it was that drove it. Boredom?

Spontaneity? Fear? Whatever it was, Molly accepted his justification for each upheaval with good grace and wholehearted support for her husband. Today she felt the usual trepidation and concern for their future and had busied herself with all that needed doing in order to supress her fears. It will be alright. We've survived this before and we will adapt. We can do it again, I know we can.

The footpath she walked along to her friend's house was a path she had followed many times over the last three years but now she was knocking on Diana's front door for one last time. Diana, answered, wiping her hands dry on a tea towel as she welcomed Molly in.

'Hello Molly. Come in for a minute. The girls are upstairs.'

'Lizzie. Becky. Mummy's here.' Diana stood on the bottom stair and called upwards to her own daughter's room where the three girls were playing together and chatting.

'How's everything going Molly? All packed up?'

'Yes. The removal van has gone and Ed's just seeing to the last few things. We're very nearly ready.'

'Well, I hope the move is a great success for you all.'

Diana was sincere and would miss her friend greatly. She was also intuitive and knew that Molly would not openly admit her reservations about another disruption to their family life.

'Thank you. I'm sure it will be. And thanks for having the girls last night. It just made everything so much easier.'

'You will ring or write when you get settled in, then? Let me know how you're getting on?'

'Of course I will.'

Molly smiled. There was no embrace between the women even though they had been good friends for the last three years.

Lizzie, aged thirteen, and Becky, her ten year old sister, ran down the staircase, followed by Judith, Diana's daughter.

'Shoes on girls, please. Daddy's waiting.'

The sisters, with shoes suitably fastened, opened the door and made their way along the footpath to their, now former, home. Molly followed, carrying the girls' overnight bags and waving and calling goodbye to Diana and Judith. Diana stood in the doorway, her arm around her daughter's shoulder, smiling weakly and watching her friend depart. She wondered how she would feel if her own husband rebranded family upheaval as 'exciting opportunities'. Molly has had to leave her job, Lizzie and Becky have had to say goodbye to their classmates and I have lost a good friend, thought Diana. I'm pretty sure I would have put up some kind of resistance if I were in Molly's shoes. She guided Judith back into the house, closed the front door gently and choked back a wave of sadness which was washing up from her chest.

By the time Molly and the girls got back, Edward was standing by the side of the car, all four doors open ready for his family to get in.

'Here we go everyone' Edward said brightly putting the girls' bags into the boot and closing it with only just enough force to ensure its secure fastening.

He shut Molly's door behind her and checked his daughters were also safely aboard.

'Where's Pinky Pig?' asked Becky in an alarmed tone, suddenly realising that her favourite soft toy was not visible.

'Oh dear. Do you really need that now?' asked an irritated Molly.

'Yes, I do.'

'Hang on Ed. Let me just get Pinky out of the boot. It's in one of those bags.'

Molly got out of the car again and lifted the boot lid to extract the errant porcine toy.

'Stinky Pinky,' teased Lizzie. 'Stinky stinky stinky.'

'He doesn't stink,' retorted Becky, jumping to the unnecessary defence of an inanimate object. 'You stink.'

'Of course he stinks,' said Lizzie. 'He's a pig, in case you hadn't noticed. Stinky stinky stinky pig.'

Becky began to cry as Molly handed her the precious soft, pink comforting bundle of fabric and stuffing.

'Cry baby,' said Lizzie and turned away from her sister to look out of the car window.

'Oh for goodness sakes stop it you two. This will be a wonderful journey if we have to listen to you two arguing all the way.' Molly shut her car door with slightly more force than was necessary and picked up the road atlas from the footwell, indicating to Edward that it was time to get going.

Edward started the engine and pulled left out of the driveway onto Winchester Road. He ignored the piggy drama going on in the back seat and focused on what would lie ahead. He glanced briefly across to Molly and saw that she had opened the map on the first page and was running her index finger slowly and deliberately along a yellow stripe which indicated the sand on their nearest bit of coastline. They would commence their northward bound journey via a red 'A' road three miles north of that. Edward had already rehearsed the route in his head and knew that he was now heading in the direction of greatness and subsequent adulation. Molly glanced briefly back at the house and she fought back the tears which were welling in her eyes. She blinked hard and looked back down at the map.

4

At thirteen years of age, Lizzie was the elder of the two sisters. A shy and introverted child, she had failed her Eleven Plus two years previously, even though she was intelligent and perfectly capable. Molly had been extremely disappointed by the failure and made her feelings perfectly clear to her eldest daughter. For the last eighteen months, then, Elizabeth Greenacre had been attending the Secondary Modern school where, despite her shyness, she had made several friends and excelled in her academic studies. She enjoyed sport too, her long limbs lending themselves to running and high jump. The school itself was an ugly 1960's building, but it had excellent facilities and inspirational teaching staff. Lizzie had been happy and in later years would look upon her short time there with fondness.

Her ten year old sister, Becky, had recently sat the Eleven Plus herself. To Molly's relief, she had passed. Had the family remained at 186 Winchester Road, she would have soon been going to the local Grammar School, but the move to South Humberside would mean that she would be attending a junior school for four months until the end of the summer term and then moving up to the Comprehensive. Rebecca Greenacre, being the younger sibling, was more gregarious and self-confident than her sister and most of her friends were of a similar disposition. There was one friend Becky had been particularly fond of – a girl named Siobhan whose parents, in an attempt to be liberal and permissive, had raised a child who could be vicious and calculating. Outwardly self-assured, Siobhan's struggle with a lack of parental boundaries manifested itself in malevolent behaviour towards some individuals whilst forming very close friendships with others. Rebecca was on Siobhan's team, but Lizzie was most definitely not. The elder sister dreaded the occasions when Siobhan would come round after school. The insidious and spiteful comments, always made when out of earshot of Molly or

Becky, seared into Lizzie's chest until full salty tears ran down her face. Lizzie spoke to no-one about it, ashamed that she could allow herself to be so badly affected by this small aggressor, two years her junior. She was glad this move meant she would never have to face Siobhan again.

'We're going to take a small detour into to town to drop off the house keys at the Estate Agents,' explained Edward to his passengers as he pulled up at the first crossroads and set of traffic lights. He looked into the rear view mirror at his daughters. Becky had Pinky Pig clasped to her chest and was sucking her thumb. Lizzie was looking out of the window at the road junction where they had temporarily stopped. The road which ran to their right was Scratchface Lane. Lizzie and Becky always called it Scratchbum Lane. It amused their father, who had a slightly naughty side to his character, but Molly was somewhat less impressed by the 'vulgar' change of title. She could hardly chastise her daughters though as Ed's amusement endorsed it. A short distance along Scratchbum Lane was the hall where Lizzie had attended the Girl Guides meeting every Thursday. It was a group run very efficiently by a self-assured and affable Brown Owl. Lizzie and her best friend Judith were enthusiastic members, taking part in all the challenges, badge earning and outings. Only last week they were with their fellow guides in a local wood, whittling bark from sticks they had picked up and mixing flour and water together to form a sticky dough. The glutinous mixture was then affixed to the end of the stick and shoved into the fire they had lit in a small clearing. Once 'cooked', Brown Owl dished out spoonfuls of her homemade raspberry jam. The girls singed their gloves as they removed their doughy campfire bread from the sticks, broke it open and smeared on large amounts of delicious jam. The end result was, in Lizzie's and Judith's mind, a gastronomic triumph – charred and smoky on the outside, soft and sticky on the inside. They thought it was delicious. There had been several camping trips too. Last summer they had been on a five day camping trip on the edge of the South Downs where they had put up their own tents in a field covered in cowpats. Huge heavy tents with wooden poles, musty smelling canvas, thick guy ropes and no groundsheets. Then they had dug holes with spades for the makeshift toilets and foraged in the woods for sticks which they lashed together with rough twine to make suitcase stands. They went on night-time walks in the dark countryside and came back to sit around a roaring campfire, chatting and singing songs. Everyone's favourite was 'Kookaburra Sits in the old Gum Tree' which they sang in a round. One evening they returned from a walk to find some cows had broken through the fence in the next door field and flattened one of the tents. Brown Owl, pragmatic as ever, simply ushered the cows back, re-allocated the spaces in the remaining upright tents to ensure everyone got somewhere to sleep and re-pitched the tent in the morning. Today marked the end of Lizzie's Girl Guiding days.

The lights changed to green and Edward pulled away. He drove along the main road towards the town. For several hundred yards there were dying Elm trees, many marked with a big white cross to denote their demise. They carried on past a row of shops, lumped over the railway line and joined a small queue of cars at the westerly end of the High Street. Molly looked through the window of McIlroys Department Store as they trundled slowly past. It was where she had shopped for dressmaking and curtain fabric. She would leave the girls on the ground floor looking through the records so that she could immerse herself in the glorious process of choosing suitable material for her latest creative project. Rubbing the fabric between her fingers to feel the weight, holding up rolls and letting the material unravel so that she could fully appreciate the pattern, and matching swatches she already had to ensure the colours would co-ordinate. She was an adept seamstress and when she married Edward, aged twenty two, she had made her own wedding dress. In McIlroys, for ten or fifteen minutes, she would find herself enchanted by the sight, smell and feel of the fabric, while her daughters flicked through the stacks of LPs which were neatly lined up in wooden racking, in order of the artist's name. Occasionally Edward would give them some money to buy a 'Top of the Pops' record. The girl on the colourful front cover would often look as though she could have done with Molly and her dressmaking skills to run up a larger item of clothing for her. She would also sometimes be smiling, possibly amused by the ludicrous cover versions of popular music contained within. The last 'Top of the Pops' LP Lizzie and Becky had purchased featured versions of My Ding-a-Ling, Long Haired Lover from Liverpool, and Crazy Horses. All ridiculous songs in their own right, but made to sound even more absurd when covered by those earnest singers, the 'Top of the Poppers'. Especially Crazy Horses; that cover had more than its fair share of crazy. The girl on the front of that LP wasn't smiling, but instead looked slightly bemused, and Edward also rudely suggested she looked like she might have wet her knickers.

Further along the high street on the other side was the road which led down to the public library. Molly would often take her daughters in there after school as both girls were avid readers. Lizzie would sometimes pick up books written in the Initial Teaching Alphabet. She had never been taught it at school but was fascinated by the way unfamiliar symbols could still be understood.

After several minutes, Edward reached the Estate Agents, parked the car on the street and went inside, explaining that he wouldn't be long. Molly, Lizzie and Becky sat silently, watching though the shop window as Edward conversed with the man who had handled the sale of their house. Molly felt a huge lump rise in her throat as she saw Edward hand over the keys to 186 Winchester Road. She looked away quickly.

5

Neither Lizzie not Becky knew what to expect from the relocation to South Humberside, except that they would undoubtedly miss their respective friends. Their father had told them that it would be an exciting adventure full of opportunities and a chance to experience a different part of the world. Being the dutiful wife, Molly had endorsed this expectation. The sisters both looked out of the car windows as they travelled along, occasionally complaining about the fumes from lorries coming into the car when they passed through a busy town and the traffic was backed up. Edward leaned back and handed them each a clean white neatly ironed cotton handkerchief and told them to hold it over their mouths and noses. It smelled of clean linen and faintly of TCP.

Their route took them initially across the rolling chalk hills of the South Downs. The fields were singing in the spring sunshine; the plough striped earth revealing vibrant green hints of new growth and the bare hedgerows stretched along the boundaries, defining and protecting the landscape. The arable land was punctuated every so often by a grass field with grazing sheep or a cluster of farm buildings. The Downs gave way to the Home Counties where the terrain was flatter and the towns more plentiful. Progress slowed as Edward negotiated his way through the traffic in the urban areas and onward to Northamptonshire.

Molly and Edward had been married for twenty one years. Molly was five years younger than her husband, and now, aged forty two, she was at her most beautiful. She had grown out of the scrawniness of her youth, but was still slim and elegant. The perfect peach-soft clear skin of her face was framed by naturally blonde hair, which today she had held back loosely with a hairband made from brightly coloured fabric and chosen to co-ordinate her dress. She had adored Edward since the age of seventeen when they had met at work.

Initially their relationship consisted of coy glances exchanged between them but an instant mutual attraction soon manifested itself in a polite 'Hello' and a smile if they passed each other in the corridor. For several weeks Edward observed her from afar, in particular watching her ride off home on her bicycle when the office closed at the end of the day. She pedalled briskly away from the car park then free-wheeled as she cycled down the hill towards the main road, her long blonde hair, cardigan and skirt flowing out behind her as she picked up speed and then turned the corner out of sight of her admirer. Finally Edward plucked up courage to ask her out and within a few weeks the tiny seed of reciprocal attraction had sprouted, grown and blossomed into genuine love. Now, two decades later, Molly's love for her husband was unshakable and she willingly dedicated herself to nurturing and supporting him in whatever he decided to do, even at the expense of her own comfort or ambition. The move which was taking place today was one such instance of a mismatch between Mr and Mrs Greenacre's desires, and yet Molly would not outwardly challenge or question her husband's decision. There would be no discord, no argument, nor abrogation of her wedding vows.

    For Edward, as each mile passed, the imagined framework of their new life was becoming more detailed. Layers of positive images were constructing a scene in which he would provide a prosperous lifestyle for his family and where his colleagues would revere him for his prodigious knowledge, his ability to lead and his strong work ethic. In his mind, their current latitudinal progress was synonymous with the Greenacre's family rise to greatness; financially, intellectually and spiritually. Not once did he look back from where they had commenced this journey. It had no relevance now. It was all about the future. Forward looking. Forward thinking. An optimistic attitude. These traits moulded Edward into the man he proudly was, and always would be. He was an adventurer with his mind set on future possibilities and opportunities. He was no stick-in-the-mud. He was a living branch of a thriving and stately oak tree, stretching out towards the sky, growing ever upwards and reaching out to the light, the sunshine and the air, and today there was so much verdant promise in his magnificent spring lushness.

Molly, meanwhile, kept her stinging eyes mainly fixed on the road map, glancing up every now and then to ensure that the snaking red line correlated with the road signs and with Edward's right and left turns. As they travelled northwards, the south coast was becoming more distant and the unknown area of South Humberside was becoming more of an uncertain and somewhat daunting reality. Their journey would take them across six pages of the road atlas. Can this really be happening again? thought Molly. She had worked hard, so hard, to get the garden and house in order. I love that house. She had nurtured the vegetables in the garden to provide delicious food for her family and she had tended the shrubs and perennials so that they had a beautiful outside area to enjoy. Digging out the brambles and ground elder left by the previous occupant was back-breaking work but she was determined to do it. I did it. The whole lot. On my own. She had grabbed tirelessly at brambles despite the thorns piercing her gloves and the tearing the sleeves of her jacket. She had dug until her knees and shoulders were searing and could take no more. In just three years she had transformed that overgrown abandoned wilderness into a vibrant and productive garden. My own little piece of paradise. She decorated the girls' bedrooms and made curtains for the large downstairs windows, choosing the fabric carefully, lining them and painstakingly hand-sewing all the hems. Now all that effort seems to count for nothing. Those achievements had nourished Molly's soul and now she was wondering if her soul might wither and shrivel. I know it's only 'bricks and mortar' but I love that house. I really do. Goodbye house, goodbye job, goodbye the comfort of familiar people and places. For better, for worse.

6

At around the half way point in their journey, Edward took a diversion from the main road and drove into a small town so that he could find somewhere to park.

'Time for a leg-stretch and a bite to eat, I'd say. What do you think?'

'Good idea,' said Molly.

'If we walk along the main street over there we'll be bound to find a tea shop.'

Edward parked in a space on the side of the street and the family got out of the car, both girls yawning and stretching as they did so. Edward locked up and they all walked towards the centre of the town scanning both sides of the shabby street for somewhere to get a late lunch. They passed a hardware shop, several grocery stores, a shoe shop, a dry cleaners and a chemist, before they found one solitary café.

'This will have to do. Come on,' said Edward, opening the door and holding it so that Molly and the girls could go in ahead of him.

The café was empty apart from one elderly lady sitting alone at a formica table in the far corner. She had a newspaper spread out in front of her and a cigarette was balanced on the edge of a glass ashtray which was already full with ash and dog ends. Her wrinkled brown hands were clasped around a tea cup, which she moved shakily to her mouth every now and then, alternating with deep drags on the cigarette.

'Let's sit here,' said Molly choosing the least dirty of the tables and pulling out a wooden chair, scraping the legs noisily along the grimy floor as she did so.

The family sat down and gingerly passed round a tatty menu which was smeared with greasy fingerprints.

A large surly man, wearing a stained apron and carrying a small notebook and pencil approached their table and asked them what they would like to drink.

'We'll have tea I think. Would you like tea too girls?' asked Edward

Lizzie and Becky replied that they would.

'Can we have a pot of tea for four then please?' he asked the waiter.

'And may we order some sandwiches as well?'

'Lunch is finished now. Sorry,' said the waiter, who didn't sound sorry at all.

'Oh dear. So there's nothing you can get us now in the way of food?'

'Cook's gone home but I can do you a fried egg sandwich.'

'Well, that will be alright. Four of your finest fried egg sandwiches please Sir,' Edward quipped, trying to keep the mood light.

The tea was passable, but as they walked back to the car, Edward remarked that this establishment was not going to be winning any awards for its gastronomic offerings.

7

The house was a shabby terraced council house which Edward had been given by his new employer to rent. At the front of the property was a pedestrianised grass area and it faced a row of equally scruffy houses opposite. Hammonds removals had already arrived and the driver had backed in his van right up to the little picket fence at the rear of the property which enclosed the small garden. Beyond the fence was an open concrete area with a row of garages running at right angles to the houses. The two men had earlier been given a key by Edward so they had already made good progress with the unloading, and many of the Greenacre's possessions were already in their new home. But it had been a long day. Edward helped them, carrying several of the remaining smaller items inside. Molly, Lizzie and Becky looked around the house with dismay, but none of them voiced their disillusionment. They were tired and a little bewildered. With the beds already having been brought in, Molly made them up with sheets, blankets and eiderdowns she pulled from a box she had packed herself earlier in the day. She then turned her attention to the kitchen, unloading the essentials for making a cup of tea. By early evening the van was emptied and the house rammed with furniture and boxes. Edward generously tipped the two employees of Hammonds removals, shook their hands and thanked them for all their hard work. He politely raised a hand to them as he watched them drive off in the direction of their overnight stop.

'That's it. We're in!' said Edward as he came back into the house.

Edward was not completely unobservant or insensitive to his family's feelings but even now, after a long drive and with the knowledge that their new home was a far cry from their old one in terms of space, location and comfort, he was full of enthusiasm for what they could make of their new lives here. He was already imagining how they could decorate the sitting room to fit in with the furniture they had brought with them and where they might place the oil lamp he had carefully wrapped twenty four hours earlier in a copy of their old neighbour's Daily Mirror. He had also already noted some available wall space in the kitchen where he could hang some extra cupboards. And then there was the commute to work. His old route had been along a busy main road into the city and a round trip of about thirty miles, but now it would be a half hour walk or a ten minute drive at most. He was looking forward to the challenge of a new role and to meeting his colleagues. He was perhaps too gentle a man to be described as gregarious, but he was certainly sociable and companionable. It was easy for him to befriend people quickly and strangers found him approachable and kind. He was certain he would have no difficulty fitting in at his new place of work. This house is smaller than Winchester Road, but that's not all bad, he thought. There will be less cleaning and gardening to do and the fuel bills will be cheaper. And everything may look a bit drab and grey outside but that's because of the time of year. When the summer comes the trees outside will be full of leaves and that muddy grass will have greened up. Tomorrow will mark the proper start of our new lives, thought Edward. And it's going to be great.

'Shall we walk up to the fish and chip shop to get supper?' he suggested to Molly. 'I noticed one back up on the main road as we drove in.'

'I think we should,' replied Molly. 'It's a bit late to be thinking about cooking.'

'Girls,' she called. 'Come downstairs please. We're going to get fish and chips.'

Lizzie and Becky had been in their respective bedrooms sorting out their possessions. Becky had dragged her clothes out of a box labelled 'Bedroom 3' and stuffed them untidily into the wardrobe and chest of drawers. Back at the old house she had pretty flowered wallpaper on her bedroom walls, a pink carpet and curtains which matched her bedspread. The window had overlooked the large back garden with her swing and colourful plants and well-stocked fishpond, home to, amongst others, Mr Orangeface whom she had won at the funfair last summer. And she had lots of floor space on which she could empty the contents of her dolls house when it needed rearranging following a bomb blast, or new inhabitant, or winning top prize of the football pools necessitating new furniture. Bedroom 3, by contrast, was pokey and uninspiring with its plain walls and tired looking brown carpet. There wasn't even room for the dolls house and the window overlooked the run of concrete garages and the untidy back gardens of the neighbouring houses. Forlornly she placed Pinky Pig on her pillow and gave him an unconvincing pat of reassurance. Later she would need his soft little pink body and velvet trotters to help her sleep.

Lizzie, meanwhile, had started unpacking her belongings but had been distracted by last week's copy of Jackie magazine. She lay down on her bed and looked at the front cover. For a few moments she was completely lost in David Cassidy's embrace, mesmerised by his sparkling eyes which were looking right at her. At her – Elizabeth Greenacre, aged thirteen from who-knows-where, England. The magazine promised a poster, but Lizzie would not dare put this on her bedroom wall as intended. That would mean her disapproving mother would know about her connection with David and that was to be avoided at all costs. It was one of her secrets, and she had unwittingly acquired the art of secrecy as a form of self-preservation. It had seeped into her psyche as she had been growing up. David was wearing an orange t-shirt with Keep Britain Tidy written on the front. There was no evidence he had actually been litter picking while wearing it; which was just as well as it was now was gently pressed against Lizzie's fluffy lemon-coloured sweater which she had bought in C & A in the January sales a few weeks earlier. David was not singing but Lizzie could hear his tuneful melody. How could he be sure, in a world which was constantly changing? Well he didn't need to worry now, because here she was, the pretty and lovely girl he had been looking for and he was holding her with his lean tanned American arms. Lizzie looked at his hair, which was shiny clean and smelled of lemons and lilac. She was about to reach up and touch it, when the call for fish and chips came through, loud and clear from downstairs.

8

The Greenacres walked out of their new front door, through the grassy area and crossed the road at the top of the close to the small shopping precinct a short distance beyond. Lizzie and Becky were subdued and trailed several feet behind their parents until they reached the fish and chip shop. Molly noticed how all the other shops, now closed for the day, had steel security shutters across their fronts, and they were defaced with graffiti. It felt alien to her. She wondered about the kind of people who were being prevented from robbing or vandalising these businesses. Were they going to be her new neighbours? Her neighbours at Winchester Road were benign and friendly. Frank next door, Hilda and Bob the other side and the Williamsons opposite. All upstanding, honest, non-violent people. The kind of people anyone would be delighted to have as neighbours and who would walk past a shop without the urge to hurl a brick through the window. The shops she used to walk to when they lived at 186 Winchester Road were not protected in this way. Was it really only yesterday morning that she was in the bakers shop there, chatting to Mr Dobson, the smiling owner, and telling him that her husband had been offered an exciting new job and she would be moving away?

Supper purchased, the family retraced their steps and went back into their new home. They squashed in around the dining table to eat.

'We'll soon get this house straight,' said Edward as he sprinkled salt and vinegar liberally over his meal. 'I don't start my new job until Monday so over the weekend I'll be working to get us all ship-shape.'

'When do we go to school?' asked Becky.

'After the weekend. And then there's only three weeks until the Easter holidays,' Molly said.

Both girls felt apprehensive about starting new schools and their initial impressions of the industrial town in which they now found themselves had not exactly filled them with confidence.

9

The first day at Eastfield Comprehensive was nerve wracking for Lizzie. For starters, the school was massive. The corridors seemed endless and the noise from the huge amount of pupils in the playground at lunchtime was overwhelming. Everyone spoke with a different accent too, making it hard for Lizzie to always understand what was being said. Someone said that she sounded 'posh' and Lizzie thought this assessment was delivered to her in a combative tone, as though they were challenging her to defend herself. She didn't. Lizzy felt scared by the teachers too. She thought back to Mr Armstrong, her old English teacher. He was strict but approachable, and very encouraging to anyone who exhibited hard work and took pride in their studies. He used to arrive in class in a tracksuit as he also took some PE lessons. Sitting on his desk (never the chair behind it) Mr Armstrong had taught her the difference between similes and metaphors in the morning and shown her how to improve her tennis backhand in the afternoon. He was kind and enthusiastic and genuinely interested in his students and their educational potential. In comparison, most of the teachers at Eastfield Comprehensive seemed short tempered and appeared to shout a lot, especially in those long corridors.

'WALK. NO RUNNING. YOU KNOW THE RULES.'

At 3.40pm, when the bell announced the end of her first day, Lizzie made her way to the cloakroom to collect her coat. From there she was going to walk to her new home which was only just over a mile away. As she walked, she felt threatened by the hostile and unfamiliar surroundings. The pungent smell of the steelworks filled the air and litter was strewn along the paths which led down the hill on the main road and snaked round the houses on the estate. David Cassidy would be horrified and would surely be compelled to gather it all up and dispose of it properly. Lizzie could even help him. She could hear chained-up dogs barking and the constant drone of traffic. Lizzie arrived home to an empty house and stood waiting in the sad little garden at the back door for her mother to return with Becky. A neighbouring boy of about four years old was lazily cycling around on his trike on the concrete area near the garages. He pedalled over to Lizzie when he saw her in the garden, got off his trike and stood silently staring at her across the picket fence. Lizzie observed his filthy hands, ragged jumper and dirty nose.

Becky's day had been confusing. Different classrooms, different teachers, different pupils. She felt out of place in her hand-knitted jumper which had been crafted by her grandmother after Molly had said that it would not be worth buying the 'official' uniform. After all, Becky was only going to be at that school for three months before moving on to the Comprehensive. She had reluctantly eaten the unpalatable school lunch then stood alone in the playground afterwards while the other children ran around chaotically, shouting loudly in their strange voices. After the final bell, Molly met her at the school gate and they walked home in the sulphurous air, passing the litter, graffiti and gawdy shop fronts, just as Lizzie had done.

'Hello Lizzie,' said Molly as they reached the back garden.

'Can you just hold Becky's bag for me please while I find my keys?'

Molly reached down into her handbag, unlocked the back door and they entered the shabby, but at least now tidy, kitchen.

'Right girls. Upstairs please and change out of your school clothes.'

Molly busied herself in the kitchen, peeling potatoes, glazing a meat pie which she had prepared earlier and chopping vegetables. She was a good cook and liked to ensure her family were properly fed with wholesome food. Fortunately the teak dining table which had brought with them when they moved had folding leaves. In this small house only one leaf was extended, but all four family members could just about squeeze in around it. Their old house was a triumph of 1960s architecture, with its large 'L' shaped sitting-come-dining room. This house by comparison had just one small sitting room and the table was squashed into a corner. While the girls had been at school and Edward had been at work, Molly had worked hard at unpacking some more boxes and trying to make the small room as usable as she could. It was clear she had to make choices about what to unpack and what to leave in boxes that would have to be stored in the garage or in the loft. On the 'unpack' side she had boxes marked 'Best Cutlery and China', Glassware, and 'Tablecloths and Napkins'. Put to one side, ready for storage, were 'Guide Books and Maps, Wedgwood, and 'Vases'. Molly had found having to make such choices rather depressing, but she knew it had to be done so she just got on with it and by early afternoon, when she stood back to look at her achievements, she had to admit they had made a big difference to the appearance of the room.

Now, in the kitchen, the timer pinged, signifying that it was time to get the pie in the oven. Molly opened the oven door, put in the pie and glanced at the clock which Edward had hung on the wall yesterday. She washed her hands, and walked along the narrow hallway which led from the kitchen to the front door. She stood, drying her hands on a towel and called up the stairs.

'Lizzie. Becky. When you're done up there can you come and set the table please? Mats are on the sideboard and the knives and forks are in that drawer underneath. And use the green tablecloth.'

Molly had learned the art of good cooking from her own mother, Phyllis. Nanna Phil was an old-fashioned plain cook but could rustle up a sponge cake or a tray of Yorkshire Puddings in the blink of an eye. And they would taste delicious. The meat pie Molly had made this evening was her mother's recipe. Nanna Phil would have worked quickly mixing lard into flour for the pastry using an old steel knife which had string round its wooden handle. What seemed like a tiny amount of braising steak and kidney would be cooked separately in the oven first and the meat juices mixed with flour and lots of white pepper to make thick gravy. The end result was a gastronomic triumph. Molly knew, when she dished up this evening, there would be the inevitable family joke about her pie being nice, but not a patch on Nanna Phil's. Molly may have inherited her mother's ability to cook, but that was the only similarity between them. Phyllis had been hardened by a tough life. Molly's father, Reginald, suffered with ill health, leaving him unable to work. Phyllis became the breadwinner, toiling for hours on end in a dirty factory and trying to bring up Molly and her two younger siblings at the same time. When war broke out houses around them were bombed and her husband's poor physical condition meant that they were often unable to get down into the air raid shelter when the siren sounded. They would hide in the cupboard under the stairs instead, praying for the danger to pass. Molly was fourteen when the war ended, emerging from the ordeal apparently unscathed. Three years on and she would meet Edward, a tall, kind, generous, good looking man with impeccable manners and of whom Phyllis and Reginald entirely approved. Molly and Edward married five years later and thus began Molly's dedication to her calling. On Molly's part it would mean sacrifices, rather than compromise, but this was what she was wholeheartedly prepared to do for the sake of her adored husband.

Around 6.00pm Edward arrived home, and the Greenacre family sat down together to eat.

'How's your first day been?' Molly enquired as she passed him a plate with a generous slice of pie.

'Thank you. Yes, not too bad at all. I've had a tour of the offices, been introduced to the top man and got my desk organised. Tomorrow I will be out and about with Malcolm taking a look at some current projects the department is working on.'

'Malcolm? Was he one of the men on the interview panel?'

'That's him, yes. Seems like a thoroughly nice chap. A refreshing change after that idiot I was working with before.'

Molly passed Edward a terrine containing potatoes.

'Lizzie. You forgot to get serving spoons out,' Molly said.

She squeezed past the back of Becky's chair and reached over to the drawer of the sideboard to obtain the forgotten spoons and placed them on the table in front of her husband.

'And did you leave enough time to get there this morning?'

'Plenty. It's about two and a half miles door to door and there's a staff car park with ample spaces. Like I said though, I'll walk most days. Oh, and just across the road from the car park is The Queen's Head. According to Malcolm it's the watering hole of choice on a Friday lunchtime.'

'What about the other people in your office? Did you get a chance to speak to them?' asked Molly as she poured gravy over her pie.

'Yes. I met most of them this morning. A good bunch, I think.'

'I'm pleased, Ed. Sounds like it's going to work out very well.'

10

By the middle of Edward's second week at the Council, he had been charged with the task of surveying a specific area of the authority's social housing stock with a view to getting them upgraded. Much of the council housing in the city had been built in the years between the two world wars and was now very much in need of updating. His role would be to visit a prescribed number of properties, assess them and report back to his superiors on what was required. He would be working in conjunction with a colleague. The colleague in question was Mayhew. At their first meeting Mayhew had seemed friendly enough, albeit less enthusiastic than Edward about the task ahead of them.

Edward was pleased that he had taken on this work at the Council and he enjoyed the responsibility and the sense of power it had bestowed on him. Unfortunately Mayhew might be lazy and unhelpful sometimes, and that impacted on Edward's workload but Ed soon worked out that his colleague had good days and bad days and on the bad days Mayhew was best left to stew about whatever it was that was causing his disagreeable mood. On the good days they worked well together, talking to tenants, assessing the required works and recording their findings which would form the basis of their recommendations. At the end of the day they would call in to the Administration Office and give their handwritten reports to Elsie, a friendly colleague who efficiently typed up their notes and brought them back the following day.

In the main office, where Edward's desk was situated, there was a less genial colleague who was a friend of Mayhew's. He could be rude and bad mannered.

Two of a kind, thought Edward; they both rubbed him up the wrong way.

Edward didn't display his irritation with these colleagues though, or regret his decision to take on take up this new employment. Edward was an optimist and was always looking to the future. Optimism was a great leveller. He knew the past could not be changed and despite some small difficulties with his new colleagues, Edward remained polite and diligent, striving, as ever, to be a good employee and a perfect gentleman. When things did really get to him he knew he could go home and impart his troubles to his ever supportive wife.

11

Right from the start of her days at Eastfield comprehensive, Lizzie experienced problems at school. She was the 'new girl'. Again. The outsider who wasn't welcome. During her second week at the school and while walking one morning along the busy road that led up to the entrance, she heard the noise of bicycle wheels on the pavement rapidly approaching from behind her. She turned to see a girl she recognised from a higher year pedalling up the hill.

This particular girl had been standing at the end of a row of lockers one day last week, deliberately preventing Lizzie from being able to reach her own and forcing her to walk up an adjacent row and back round. Now here she was again and she was cycling so fast she would soon be level with Lizzie.

Feeling scared, Lizzie turned back round, quickened her pace and prayed that nothing was about to happen. As the girl drew level, Lizzie heard her spit. Terrified of what she might find, she waited until the girl was several metres further up the hill before stopping and pulling her satchel off her shoulders to examine it. There was nothing. Lizzie then removed her coat and found saliva dripping down the back. She was disgusted. She had nothing to wipe it off with and stood for several seconds wondering what she should do.

She decided the best course of action would be to scrape the coat against the rough bark of a large tree which was one of several lining the side of the road. Shaking, due to the cold air and possibly the fear she was feeling, Lizzie managed to wipe the coat reasonably clean before putting it back on and continuing her way to school.

For the rest of the day, Lizzie was cautious, looking out for her aggressor when she had cause to walk those long corridors or when she was outside in the playground at lunchtime.

It turned out the girl had several accomplices who regularly picked on younger girls and boys. They seemed to have an ability to sniff out pupils who they perceived as being weak and it appeared to Lizzie that they got perverse pleasure from exerting power over their victims.

Lizzie watched them name-calling, hair-pulling, obstructing and indulging in various other unpleasant activities. She was frightened when she was the one on the receiving end of this nasty behaviour and disgusted with herself for being relieved when she saw it being dished out against someone else.

In those first two weeks, Lizzie was reticent to make friends with anyone as she hadn't worked out who she could trust. There was just one girl who took the initiative and befriended Lizzie. Her name was Helen and she shared a love of art with her new friend.

They sat next to each other in their art class, and over the coming weeks, they would be experimenting with mixing paints, creating miniature sculptures by carving soap bars with scalpels, cutting coloured sugar paper to make mosaic images and scrubbing charcoal on to card then smudging it out with their fingers. It was clear from the outset that Lizzie and her art buddy would become firm friends.

Helen lived at the 'better' side of town and, at the end of the second week, invited Lizzie to call round on Saturday. Lizzie was happy to accept the invitation. The two girls spent time playing Bowie, Elton John and Slade at forty five revolutions per minute on a little record player which belonged to Helen's older brother.

Then they took a walk through the grim but busy shopping arcade in the centre of town, stopping in Woolworths to get their photograph taken in a photo booth.

Lizzie kept the photo and years later she would look at the little monochrome image, note the smiling teenage faces and the juvenile but neat handwriting on the reverse. 'Helen and Lizzie – March 1973' it read. She would look at the bright eyes and the long shiny hair with centre partings. She would try hard to recall the happy phases of that time in her life.

Despite Lizzie's new friendship, in the main, both she and her sister felt bewildered and unsettled in their new surroundings, and Molly was trying hard, but failing, to make 78 Wordsworth Close feel like home.

Edward was striving to fulfil his duties at the council to the best of his ability. The family were continuing to function with their everyday responsibilities but they were already beginning to feel forlorn and miserable, and it was only week three.

Even the optimistic Edward doubted his decision to move to this unattractive town, with more than its fair share of dour people and its putrid air. Having his car roof stoved in by some snotty kid who had run along the row of garages at the back of the house then jumped down onto his vehicle hadn't helped with his appraisal of his own ability to improve his quality of life. Neither had the alarming discovery of something decidedly suspicious on a Saturday morning just a few days later.

12

'Molly, I'm going to fix that creaking board in the hall floor. Will I be in your way if I do it now?'

'Not at all. I'm about to go across to the shops and get a few bits and pieces and something for dinner tonight and lunch tomorrow. I'll go to the butchers and get a shoulder of lamb, I think.'

'Oh lovely. Do we have mint sauce?'

Molly wrote the requested condiment down on her shopping list and checked in her purse to ensure she had enough money for the groceries. 'I won't be long.'

'Bye dear. I'll make a start here then. About time I mended it. It's been making a dreadful racket ever since we moved in.'

Molly left by the back door and Edward set to work, kneeling down and carefully easing the carpet from the gripper, folding it back neatly so that he could examine the offending board. He found a couple of nails helpfully protruding and deftly removed them with a claw hammer. Edward noted that all the adjoining floorboards were firmly fastened and would not need any attention. He pulled up the board which was going to require fixing and as he did so, something in the floor cavity below caught his eye. It was a small cloth bag, obviously with something in it. Edward reached down, picked up the bag and opened it. Inside he found a leather wallet, empty except for a dry cleaning ticket, a small carriage clock and several items of ladies jewellery. He examined each piece in turn then placed them back into the bag. Puzzled, he looked back down into the hole where he saw a couple of jemmies, some wire cutters, a knife and a large chisel. Now he realised what this was about. Nervously he replaced the bag on top of the tools and put the board back temporarily over the gap to conceal the items about which he was beginning to feel increasingly uneasy. For a second or two he sat back on his haunches and tried to assimilate what he had just seen. Getting rather unsteadily to his feet, he went into the kitchen, made himself a cup of coffee and sat down to drink it in the sitting room. The person responsible for what he had just found had obviously once lived in this very same house. He could have made coffee in the kitchen, as Edward himself had just done and could have sat in the room where Edward now was. Presumably he would have slept in one of the bedrooms where his family now slept. Edward found those thoughts slightly disturbing. Certainly changing the locks on the doors would be a priority. He drank his coffee slowly and pensively then went out into the back garden and stood in the cold air, looking at the dreary row of concrete garages and the block of equally unattractive houses opposite. He stood still, thinking for several minutes about what his next course of action should be.

'Oh, hello Ed. Whatever are you doing standing out here? It's freezing,' said Molly as she returned home and reached over to open the back garden gate.

Edward took the heavy shopping bag from her hands.

'I want you come and see something Molly. Tell me what you think.'

'What is it?' asked a concerned Molly.

'You'll see,' said Edward as he walked back into the house. 'Follow me.'

Edward put the bag of shopping down on the kitchen worktop and led Molly into the hallway.

'Look here,' Edward said as he lifted the floorboard once more and pulled out the bag.'

'There's a clock, these earrings, bracelets, rings and a wallet. Unsurprisingly empty. And look what I found underneath,' said Edward pointing down towards the floor cavity.

'Oh dear, Ed,' said Molly. She stood for a second or two, peering down into the space between the floorboards. 'I would say someone's stolen property and the 'tools of the trade'. What do you think we should do? Report it to the police?'

'Yes, I think we'd better, don't you?'

'Do you know where the station is?'

'Top end of Ashby Street. I'll make my way down there fairly soon.

'I wonder how long those things have been there.' Molly said.

'Not long.' Edward reached into the bag he was still holding and fetched out the wallet. Look at the date on this dry cleaning ticket.'

Molly took the ticket. 'Ready by 15 February 1972. Only just over a year ago. So do you think whoever lived here before us is responsible?'

'That would be my guess,' said Edward. 'Someone has been robbed of their possessions. So we must report it.'

'Probably all we can do, Ed. We can't just leave those things there and we certainly can't dispose of them. Oh Ed. This is not nice. It makes me feel a bit uncomfortable to think that over the last few weeks we've walked across those things lots of times, having no idea they were down there.'

'I know what you mean,' Edward replied as he dropped the bag back into the hole.

'Anyway, you go and unpack the shopping. I'll just move things back here so we don't do ourselves an injury. I'll come and give you a hand in a minute then get down into Ashby Street.'

Molly moved through into the kitchen to being unpacking. Edward replaced the floorboard and carpet then stored his toolbox in the cupboard under the stairs.

'I wonder why those things were left there,' said Edward as he joined Molly in the kitchen. 'Do you suppose he left in a hurry? Surely you wouldn't forget that you had left stuff like that hidden under floorboards would you?'

Edward took a cauliflower and a bag of carrots from the shopping bag and put them on the worktop.

It's very odd Molly. Very odd indeed.'

'Maybe he was arrested and didn't have an opportunity to retrieve them,' Molly ventured.

'Possibly.'

Edward took the remaining items from the bag and hung the shopping bag back on the hook by the kitchen door.

'I'll get off now. If I time it right I can pick the girls up from the cinema on the way back to save a second journey.'

He lifted his jacket from the end of the bannister and felt in his pocket for the car keys.

'I'll see you later,' said Edward as he picked up his gloves from the kitchen worktop and kissed his wife on the cheek. 'Lock the door behind me as I go out. I'll buy some new locks too while I am in town.'

Slowly and carefully Edward reversed his vehicle out of his allotted drab grey garage, then turned right out of the close onto the main road which led into town. The traffic lights at the junction with Mill Street turned red as he approached. He slowed his car to a gentle stop. As he sat waiting for amber and green to appear, he considered both perpetrator and victim. There had been a few items of post addressed to a Mr S Thompkins arrive at their house since they moved in. Edward had simply written 'Not at this Address. Return to Sender' across the front of the envelopes and put them back into the post box. Could S Thompkins be the person who had broken into someone else's home, invaded their privacy, taken valuable items and left them feeling vulnerable and upset? He had been driven to break the law, but why? And after going to the all the trouble of purloining those items they had just been left hidden under the floorboards, so he must have left the house in a hurry before getting a chance to sell them. Perhaps he had already been convicted of other crimes or maybe he was still at large, undetected and persisting in robbing others. And what about the legitimate owner of those items of jewellery? Was she frightened and heartbroken after realising someone had smashed through a window in the middle of the night and taken her belongings? The jewellery must have had sentimental as well as intrinsic value. It had probably been given to her by a much loved husband, mother or sibling. Edward thought about the jewellery he had given Molly over the years, in particular the platinum and gold engagement ring with its two diamonds set diagonally opposite each other. Molly had been twenty one years old when, after seeking permission from her father, Edward had placed the ring on her finger and proposed to her. It was a symbol of his undying love for her. Imagine if someone were to take that away from her now, two decades later. She would be extremely distressed.

The lights signalled go and Edward drove on. Within a few minutes he had reached the end of Ashby Street and he turned into the Police Station forecourt, reversing into a vacant spot in the front row of spaces. He walked up the three steps leading to the large entrance door, went inside and gave all the details to the Officer behind the desk.

13

With its Art Deco façade fading and pale yellow paint peeling from the walls, the local cinema looked a rather uninspiring place to spend nearly three hours on a Saturday morning. However, inside, and waiting for the main film to start, were about three hundred noisy and excitable children. They were whirling around the cinema, running back and forth to the lavatories, calling over to their friends several rows away, changing seats as the whim took them and throwing wrapped boiled sweets to each other. The cinema attendants made no effort to control the mayhem. They had become accustomed to this Saturday morning madness and it was accepted as perfectly normal behaviour. Lizzie, Helen and Becky were among the throng but had now decided which seats to sit in. Lizzie had a bag of chocolate limes in her lap and Becky had barley sugars. They were sharing them with Helen. From her seat, Lizzie was anxiously looking around to ensure none of the 'nasty' gang from school were anywhere near her. She was relieved to find that there was no evidence of them at all this morning. Today's main screening was Bedknobs and Broomsticks – a fantasy wartime story involving evacuation, witchcraft and ultimate defeat of the Nazis. The audience settled down as the film started but throughout there was the hum of voices and rattling of sweet wrappers. The finer intricacies of the storyline were perhaps a little bewildering for the younger viewers, but there was plenty of colour and music to keep their interest. Becky especially enjoyed the magical underwater scene and the silly song which accompanied it: *Bobbing along, Singing a Song, on the bottom of the Beautiful Briny, Shimmering Shiny, Beautiful Briny Sea.* For two hours Lizzie and Becky forgot about all about the awfulness which had presented itself to them in recent weeks. They were swathed in an entrancing musical mantle, wrapped up and temporarily given respite from their childhood concerns.

14

Molly worked swiftly in the kitchen. If Ed was stopping to buy some new door locks from the ironmongers, and picking up the girls from the cinema on his way back from the police station, then she would have this evening's meal prepared and ready to cook later by the time they all got back. She deftly peeled and chopped vegetables and put the seasoned meat into a dish, covering it with foil. She thought about Ed's discovery this morning and hoped the matter would soon be resolved. She didn't like the thought of stolen goods being concealed beneath her hall floor. A sudden rattle from the front door startled her. Several envelopes had been pushed through the letterbox. Molly dried her hands on a tea towel and went through to pick them up from the doormat. She flicked through them as she walked slowly back to the kitchen. One she recognised as her Mother-in-Law's handwriting and it was addressed to Edward alone. Another, also addressed to Edward, looked like it was a gas bill. There was a statement from the bank, a communication from a publications company and finally a handwritten envelope addressed to Molly. She placed the first four items on to the kitchen worktop and took the final letter through to the sitting room where she sat down to open it.

My Dear Molly

I do hope all is well with you all those miles away. I know you told me not to write to you and that I should wait until you contacted me, but it's been two weeks since I last heard from you. I know you must have been really busy unpacking and getting your house straight. Sorry. And please forgive me if I have made things difficult for you. I just wanted to let you know that I have missed your lovely company so much. I have been thinking back to our last meeting and I am wondering how long it will be before we can see each other again, or if we will even see each other again. I have been plodding on at work – it's all pretty dull at the

moment, but it pays the bills. I had a lovely walk along the seafront last weekend down to the pier and back and this weekend some colleagues have roped me in to playing darts with them. I don't really like darts, and I certainly don't possess much skill, but they made it difficult for me to say no! It's that nice little pub on the corner of Chapel Street – 'The Wagon and Horses' – you remember? I expect it will be good evening, even if I can't hit the board! Then it will be Monday again before I know it, and back to work! Anyway, please let me know how you are Molly and apologies once again for breaking the rules regarding contacting you.
 Love always,
 James

Molly put the letter back into the envelope with trembling hands then ran upstairs and put it in a box at the bottom of her wardrobe. She looked at the bedroom clock in order to assess how much time she might have before Ed's return. Just enough, she considered. Back downstairs, in the sitting room, she took out her writing paper and pen from the bureau.

Dear James
 It was so lovely to hear from you but you really must NOT write to me here. Fortunately Edward is out this morning and your letter has arrived in his absence, but that is just a lucky piece of coincidence. I too have missed you – terribly. It is awful now living so far away from you but trust me, when the time is right, we will no longer have to keep secrets. The time is just not right yet, but that day <u>will</u> come. I will write to you again properly next week or maybe even try to call you if I can. I promise.
 With much love,
 Molly

James was fragile. Molly was well aware of that fragility so hoped her letter had been written in an appropriate manner. She licked the envelope to stick it down, reached back into the bureau for a stamp, affixed that too and grabbed her shoes and coat from the hallway so that she could run across to the post box.

15

'Good evening Sir. Mr Greenacre?' A gush of Monday evening spring air sprinted into the hall as Edward opened the front door to its fullest extent.

'Yes,' replied Edward.

'My name is Officer Fransham, and this is my colleague Officer Melton. I believed you called in at the station on Saturday morning. I wonder if we could come in for a few minutes. Is it convenient?'

'Of course,' said Edward stepping back and gesturing for the Officers to make their way into the hallway of 78 Wordsworth Close. At number 83 opposite, the front room curtains had been pulled back very slightly to allow the inhabitants to observe two police officers on the doorstep of their new posh neighbours' house. Edward pretended not to notice the movement of the window dressings at number 83, but he had. Even though the Greenacre family had only resided in Wordsworth Close for four weeks, each member had begun to work out who lived where. On Lizzie's part it was a self-protection exercise - she needed to know where the enemies were. On Becky's because, being younger, she was just curious. Edward and Molly, being sociable people, were subconsciously wondering if any of their new neighbours might become friends and although neither of them had voiced their concerns to each other, they had realised fairly soon after the move that this area did not seem to contain any like-minded individuals. They weren't being snobbish. They just felt like they didn't fit in. Certainly not with the window spies at number 83. Edward had walked past their house last week and tried to make polite conversation with Mr 83 as he arrived home on a bicycle. Edward offered a cheery 'Good Afternoon' but the unenthusiastic response was a grunt as Mr 83 dismounted, spat his cigarette end on to the ground, stubbed it out with his foot and pushed his bicycle around the back. Edward wasn't even sure if the grunt was a response. It might just have been due to the effort exerted when taking a final inhalation of tobacco smoke while getting off a bike. Edward had related the story to Molly later and she told him that Mrs 83 wasn't much friendlier. Molly had recognised and smiled at Mrs 83 in the newsagents on Friday. The gesture wasn't reciprocated.

'We'll go into the sitting room,' said Edward. 'It's the door on your left there. Please, take care with the carpet. I've just it pulled back so that we can lift the floorboards. And do take a seat.' Edward closed the front door behind the officers and the curtains of number 83 resumed their usual position.

Officer Fransham sat down on the red velour settee and his colleague positioned himself next to him. Edward walked over to the sideboard and poured himself a whisky.

'Would either of you like one?'

'On duty, Sir. Otherwise it would have been lovely.'

'Yes, my apologies,' said Edward and took a sip from the tumbler. 'Cup of tea then? Coffee?'

'No thank you. I'm fine,' replied Officer Fransham.

'Not for me either, but thank you anyway,' replied his colleague.

Edward sat down on the armchair opposite his visitors and took a large sip of his whisky. 'Thank you for coming round so soon. I suppose you have been briefed on my uncovering of some interesting items under the floorboards of our hall?'

'Yes, that's right. I just need to make a few notes before we take a look in the hallway if that's alright with you Mr Greenacre.' Officer Fransham removed a small notepad and pencil from his pocket.

'Yes. Perfectly fine,' said Edward.

'Nothing too much for you to worry about, Sir. Firstly, may I ask how long you have been living here?'

'Ummmm. It was the sixteenth of March when we moved in.'

'This year?' enquired the Officer.

'Yes, this year. It's not even a month since we arrived.'

'Newcomers to the area then?'

'Yes. Still adjusting and getting settled.'

'And I understand you were doing some work to the floor in the hall which led to the discovery of some items you are concerned about. Is that correct?'

'Yes, that's right.'

'When was that Mr Greenacre?'

'On Saturday morning. About 10 o'clock, I think.'

'So that was the first time you have seen the items?'

'Correct.'

'And you have left them in situ?'

'There's a bag and some tools. I did lift the bag out and take a look inside, but the tools are left just as I found them. As soon as we realised what they were, I put the bag back, replaced the board and came straight down to your station.'

Officer Fransham recorded all the details of Edward's discovery on his notepad in bold neat handwriting. He observed that Edward was well-spoken and was smartly dressed in a dark grey suit, pale green shirt and colourful silk tie. It looked expensive. His clean hands with neatly clipped fingernails were wrapped around his whisky tumbler. His hair was dark and shiny clean and his moustache and sideburns neatly trimmed. Officer Fransham had earlier noted that it was a single malt which now filled the bottom third of the glass. Both Officers were familiar with this part of town as several of their 'clients' lived on this very estate. Only six doors down, on the same side, at number 66 was the Kirby family. Officer Fransham had paid them a visit only last week. The eldest of the numerous Kirby offspring had been caught in town late one evening with two of his mates, pulling plants from the floral displays outside the Littlewoods store and tossing them into the road at passing cars. Lizzie wasn't familiar with the boy who harnessed such strange horticultural hatred as he was four years older than her, but she had become aware of his younger brother. He was to be avoided as she travelled to and from school on account of his inability to walk for twenty five minutes without loudly yelling embarrassing obscenities at other pupils. He also had dirty teeth. On school mornings she would try and time her departure from the house so that she was either well ahead of Shouty-Boy or at least three minutes behind.

Both Officer Fransham and Officer Melton wondered why someone like Edward Greenacre was residing in this property. He didn't seem to fit the mould of Wordsworth Close. It would be completely unprofessional to ask though.

'Good. Thank you Sir,' he said as he closed his notepad and returned it to his pocket. I think what we will do is simply remove the items now and leave you to repair your floor and then enjoy the rest of your evening.'

'Well, if you need me assist in any way then shout up.'

'We should be alright, thank you.'

Both Police Officers stood up and made their way back into the hallway. Officer Melton unfolded a large bag and handed it over to his colleague. This was the last call of their shift and had not been an unpleasant experience. On their return to the station they would deal with the necessary formalities and then make their way home to their respective families. Tomorrow would probably be another day of dealing with a mixture of the manifestations of petty crime and trying to prevent it where they could. This town, however, was no stranger to more serious offences, so who could tell what tomorrow might hold.

Within a few seconds, the floorboard had been lifted and the bag and tools removed.

'Thank you Mr Greenacre. That's it.'

Edward opened the front door and smiled at both Officers. 'Goodbye both of you. Thank you very much.' He closed the door and went back to the sitting room where he topped up his whisky glass then flopped down into the armchair.

16

Now that school was finished for the Easter Break, Edward and Molly arranged a trip to Norfolk to meet up with some friends and also to visit Nanna Phil and Grandad. Edward had trained in architecture with his old friend Graham and, despite moving away to different parts of the country after qualifying, they had kept in touch, married their respective partners and each had two daughters. Graham had worked for a firm of architects for a couple of years, gained some experience and then branched out on his own, eventually setting up his own business in a small market town in North Norfolk. He had worked hard and made enough money to buy, and renovate, an old rectory in which he now lived with Suzanne, his wife, and his teenage children Caroline and Victoria. The Greenacres hadn't planned on taking a holiday so soon after the move, but there was an unspoken consensus that it was a necessary interlude in their resettling process.

'I've just spoken on the telephone to Graham. They are expecting us around four o'clock this afternoon. I think we should leave here within the next hour if we can.'

Molly finished drying up and putting away the crockery and cutlery.

'Yes, Ed dear. That's fine. I've finished here and got everything packed. Girls are just about ready. Can you bring down the suitcases from upstairs please?'

Edward carried down the cases and bags and stacked everything neatly into the back of the car which he had got out of the garage a little earlier.

This trip was going to be a welcome change from South Humberside and everything it had hurled at him over the last four weeks. He was looking forward to seeing his old friend too.

Someone who made him feel at ease and with whom he could share a few whiskies, sitting by the fire in the cosy little Old Rectory study.

Graham was more sophisticated, more well-travelled and more well-read than the men who had featured in his life recently and he was talkative without being opinionated or judgemental. He had a gentle, but slightly naughty, sense of humour which appealed to Edward. Graham was a couple of years younger than his friend and Edward liked to think that if his brother had survived, this would have been the kind of man he would have grown into. Yes, this break was going to be just the tonic he needed.

17

Bands of feathery wispy clouds caressing a massive cobalt blue sky. A glorious expanse of golden sand sweeping round a huge bay, framed by sweet smelling pinewoods and dunes. Tiny figures in the distance walking with their dogs, who were running excitedly towards the edge of the sea and then back again to their owners. A brilliant sun, lighting up the air with perfect clarity. The call of skylarks, geese and seabirds being carried on the cool salty breeze. A solitary boat making its way eastwards across the distant North Sea, which on a day like today, was calm and blue. This was where the Greenacre family found themselves twenty four hours after leaving home. Edward and Graham walked together across the sand, reminiscing about their student days and discussing their respective current careers. Molly and Suzanne strolled behind, chatting about family life and their daughters. They had a lot in common with each other, although Suzanne was less compliant in her marriage to Graham and considered her own opinions and desires to be of significant importance in their relationship. She was trying hard to raise her daughters as confident and independent young women. Those two girls were now several hundred metres away at the water's edge with Lizzie and Becky, all four girls running backwards quickly when the shallow waves broke and rolled in across the sand towards their feet. As the water receded, shiny smooth pebbles were revealed, the girls picking up those they considered the prettiest and most colourful. The families walked for a considerable distance along the bay before heading back towards the fragrant pinewoods.

Graham and Edward reached a long flight of wooden steps which would lead them up across the dunes and to a path they could follow through the woods back to the little hamlet where they had left their cars. At the bottom of the steps and on either side, was a line of brightly coloured beach huts, each sporting a whimsical or amusing name above its door. The men stopped briefly to look at them. 'Fanta-Sea', 'Seas The Day' and 'Vitamin Sea' were Edward's favourites. It struck Edward that even though this was the Easter holiday season, not many of them were in use. One hut, about ten away from where they were standing, was occupied. A young couple were sitting on the little veranda while their two young sons were on the sand below them, playing cricket with toy bats and a tennis ball. They had a golden Labrador with them who kept running off with the ball making the children laugh as they chased him round so that they could resume their game.

Edward and Molly hadn't felt this relaxed or calm for some time. Their hosts had certainly chosen a wonderful place to bring them on the first day of their visit. They realised they missed living near the coast. All seven far flung locations in which Edward and Molly had lived since their marriage had been within a short driving distance of the sea, and they had always taken advantage of that, going on blustery invigorating walks in the winter and indulging in sandcastles and picnics in the summer. Some of those beaches had been busy, noisy places in the holiday season as they filled up with tourists. Tourists who wanted ice-creams, candyfloss and funfairs and who jostled their way along promenades full of kiosks selling inflatable rafts, buckets and spades, and silly brightly coloured postcards. But the beach where they were today was different. It was so vast it would be easy to find solitude. Its beauty was breathtaking. The light was spectacular and the breeze was fresh and cool. The air pierced its way into their eager lungs and washed over their cold faces so that their cheeks became flushed.

Edward and Graham climbed the sandy steps up to the woods and turned right to follow the soft pine needle clad pathway through the trees.

'Have you heard anything from Dennis recently?' Edward asked.

'Not for some time,' replied Graham. 'I'm not sure what happened to him after Dizzy Doris walked out on him. As far as I know she took her ample charms elsewhere when she decided she'd had enough of his boozing. It's all rather sad, I'm afraid. He always was a drinker though, wasn't he? Can you remember those Friday nights we had back in Leicester? Dear God! I mean, you and I could put it away after a long week in college, but Dennis! He just didn't know when to stop. Even on his wedding day. Completely intoxicated. Everyone squirming in their seats as he made that unfortunate rambling speech about Dizzy's parents and how he was so happy to be marrying someone who had inherited her mother's physique and her father's brains. I think you and I joined in with the polite, nervous but somewhat forced laughter at the appropriate moments but inside we were horrified. Wasn't it awful? Now the poor old bugger is on his own somewhere probably, drinking himself into an early grave. I really must try and find out where he is and how he is.'

'Oh dear,' replied Edward. 'That doesn't sound good. I always thought he and Doris were a good match, so that's a shame.' Edward was always highly amused by Graham's 'Dizzy' prefix when referring to Dennis' now estranged wife, but he couldn't actually bring himself to use that moniker for her. 'Maybe she'll see reason and return. After all, she wasn't averse to a drop of the hard stuff herself, was she?'

'Not exactly,' agreed Graham. 'Talking of which, I must take you to The White Hart in town. It's the nearest public house to my office so I sometimes sneak in there for a crafty one before going home. It's an old coaching inn; a good old fashioned drinking hole, cheery landlord, nice beer, dart board and dominoes. What more could you want?

'It sounds very pleasant,' said Edward, who actually thought it sounded much more than merely very pleasant as he imagined himself and his old friend in there sitting by an inglenook fireplace, drinking pints, laughing and patting the soft heads of winsome brown-eyed border collies who were sitting obediently and serenely by their masters' sides.

'Let's see if we can squeeze in a visit there tomorrow,' volunteered Graham. 'Although we'll have to see if the ladies have anything else planned,' he continued, suddenly remembering that his plans were quite often constrained by his organised wife and what she might have already arranged.

The two men continued their walk through the meandering path under the canopy of the tall pine trees. Dappled light fell in golden pools through the branches onto the undulating ground and, in the far distance, occasionally visible to their right hand side on the other side of the dunes, the North Sea was washing its way along the width of the broad sandy bay as the tide came slowly in. Every few minutes they would pass people walking in the opposite direction; Graham and Edward said a polite 'Good Morning' which was reciprocated with the same greeting. If they had a dog with them Edward would hold out his hand and click his tongue in canine greeting, but the dogs took no notice, their noses to the ground and their eyes and ears alert to the smorgasbord of aromas, sounds and sights which consumed their simple fervent spirits.

'Back to the house for lunch then. You better follow me Ed,' said Graham as they reached their vehicles and he unlocked the door of his large Rover.

'Yes. Don't drive too fast!' replied his guest, whose cautiousness in some areas of his life was in stark contrast to others.

18

Back at the Old Rectory, Suzanne took out large joint of slow cooked roast beef from the shiny dark blue Aga and placed it on the wooden kitchen table to rest. Molly helped her to chop vegetables and make the gravy. Meanwhile, all four girls made their way into the dining room to set the table. The huge antique mahogany dining table which dominated the room reflected the sunlight coming through one of the large sash windows. On the far side of the room was an ornate Victorian fireplace with a mantelpiece above, on which sat a pair of silver candlesticks, a vase containing a beautiful flower arrangement and several items of expensive coloured glassware. The floorboards were dark and polished and a large deep red Persian wool rug covered the centre of the room. Coordinating full length drapes hung at the windows and an elaborate glass light fitting hung grandly from the high ceiling. Copious amounts of artwork were displayed on the walls, some depicting pleasing rural idyllic scenes, whilst others were carefully crafted botanical images or life drawings of curvaceous women. Suzanne had been to art college in her late teens and had a flair for painting and interior design. The room in which they were all about to sit down and share a delicious lunch was testament to her creative talents.

'How's everything with your parents?' asked Suzanne as she passed Molly a saucepan in which to put the carrots.

'They keep on going … you know … Dad's condition is worsening but it's been such a gradual process that Mum has always just adapted to it as they've gone along.'

'Your Mum is such a great support to him, isn't she? Must be hard though.'

'Oh yes, it's really difficult. We're going to see them on Tuesday.'

Molly handed Suzanne the saucepan of carrots. She set it on to the hotplate of the Aga and poured over some boiling water.

'Mum's strong though,' continued Molly. 'Rose helps out quite a bit, but in the main Mum just gets on with things.'

'Can you pass me that spoon please?'

Molly handed Suzanne the wooden spoon she had pointed to and Suzanne used it to slowly stir the pan of rich, thick, simmering gravy which had earlier been enriched with a good glug of red wine.

'Rose still lives in the same street?'

'Never moved. I'm lucky to have my sister on hand for Dad. Not so easy for me living so far away.'

'A kind and loving sister. How fortunate you are Molly.'

Molly knew that Suzanne didn't enjoy a good relationship with her own sister and wasn't sure if she should ask Suzanne about her.

'Have you seen much of Nanette recently?' asked Molly tentatively, wiping up some splashes of water from the top of the Aga with a tea towel.

'Cut all contact now, I'm afraid.' Suzanne turned her attention to the cabbage which needed moving across on to the other hotplate.

'I tried so hard to keep things on friendly terms – for the girls' sake really. After all, she is their only Auntie. And she plays the part of being a good Auntie too. Always on her terms, you know, and I wonder what would happen if they asked her for help of any kind. She has a tendency to drop friends who develop what she regards as problems. Life has to be perfect, you see. I have just got so fed up with her dreadful judgemental attitude. And that subtle vindictiveness, especially towards Graham.'

'What on earth has she got against Graham?'

'I have no idea. She's just never liked him. Not that she's ever admitted it directly, of course. It's all more insidious than that. She'll invite me to her home, to a restaurant, out shopping – always just me on my own. Graham doesn't get included.'

Suzanne reached into a cupboard and fetched out a little glass mustard pot and handed it to Molly.

'Can you mix me up some mustard and put it there for me?

She passed Molly a tin of mustard and a spoon.

'We've only once had an invitation as a couple. It's very bad mannered. And worse still she feeds my poor old father lies about him – stealthily drips them in, bit by bit, and so he's taken against Graham now too. That was the final straw for me.'

Molly felt sorry that Suzanne didn't get on with her only sibling and she could see that for such a strong, independent and capable woman, the breakdown of the sisterly relationship had had a significant effect on her. Thank goodness I have Rose. Lovely Rose. My kind, beautiful sister.

'Do you think Nanette is jealous of you?'

'Could be. I suppose. Never really thought of it like that as she has such a superior attitude. Like she's trying to make me feel jealous of her all the time.'

'What's her husband like?'

'Alright. But totally under her control now. I mean TOTALLY. He's been conditioned to say the same absurd things, like the same things, even think the same way. He's turned into a male version of her. And he seems scared of her almost. It's a bit pathetic. I really do think she's shot herself in the foot with him. If there ever comes a point in her life where she needs to rely on him, he won't be able to give her any support. He can't think for himself anymore.'

Suzanne reached behind her and grabbed a bottle of gin.

'Anyway, enough of my moaning. Pass me those glasses and slice up a lemon for me, would you? We'll have a G and T while the vegetables are finishing off.'

Back in the dining room, the girls were setting out eight places on the table with mats, cutlery and glasses.

'You've got the knife and fork round the wrong way, silly,' said Lizzie at one point, correcting her younger sister's efforts to place the cutlery.

Caroline gave Becky a pile of white linen napkins and some silver napkin rings.

'Here. Help me do these instead. You've just got to roll them up nice and tight and stick them in these.'

Becky followed Caroline's instructions as best she could but was distracted by Victoria hanging on to the back of one of the dining chairs and practising her fondu and plié ballet moves.

'Can I do that?'

'Come here then,' said Victoria.

'Hold on to the middle rail of this chair. That's it. Now, feet in first position.'

Victoria bent down in front of Becky and pulled her feet round.

'That's it. Now, watch me.'

Victoria performed a well-practised and elegant plié in front of her student and Becky attempted to copy her.

'Your bum's sticking out, Becky' laughed Lizzie.

'So's yours. And you're not even doing ballet.'

'Graham and Ed,' called Suzanne from the kitchen door when the vegetables were cooked and placed into the serving dishes which had been warming in the Aga. 'Lunch is ready.'

Everyone made their way into the dining room and sat down ready to eat.

'I know you're off to see your parents on Tuesday but what would you like to do tomorrow?' Suzanne asked as she passed across a terrine of roast potatoes to Molly. 'I thought we might go into the city in the afternoon, take a walk round the museum and do a bit of shopping too, if you want.'

'That sounds good,' said Molly, even though she wasn't sure if their finances would stretch to much shopping. It was not something she particularly enjoyed and anyway, she was fairly sure there had been a lot of expense incurred with their recent house move.

'What a lovely idea,' said Edward. 'I would love to visit the city and the museum. I'm sure Molly and the girls would too. We will have dinner out afterwards. And I am paying. It's my way of thanking you for being such charming and gracious hosts.' He picked up the glass of red wine that Graham had just poured for him. 'Here's to friendship, good health and the future.'

Graham raised his glass and returned the sentiment, confident that, by default, he now had clearance to take his old friend into town in the morning.

19

Graham parked his Rover in the market place car park. Edward got out and pushed the heavy passenger door closed. It was mid-morning and the Norfolk spring air was already warm. The sky was crystal clear save for one thin wisp of high cloud which stretched fuzzily from east to west. Elegant eighteenth and nineteenth century buildings surrounded the little market square. On the sunlit side of the square a florist had put out buckets full of fresh flowers and placed them artistically on the pavement beneath his shop front and the overhanging striped sunblind. Next door a greengrocer had also neatly loaded his display boxes full of cabbages, potatoes, onions, and carrots on the right hand side of his shop doorway and on the left were apples, bananas, oranges and grapes. On the opposite shady side of the square was a wool shop. The colours of the yarns displayed beautifully in the shop window echoed the fruit and vegetables on the other side. Edward found the symmetry gratifying. A red post box stood between the wool shop and the newsagent next door. Edward noticed a bicycle propped up against it. Adjoining the newsagents was a bakers shop with a tapestry of loaves, rolls and cakes laid out attractively to entice customers inside. Even from several metres away, Edward could smell the intoxicating aroma of freshly baked bread. In the far corner of the market place was The White Hart, just as Graham had promised.

Graham locked the Rover and gestured towards the opposite corner from The White Hart. 'My office is just over there.'

The two men crossed the road and, on reaching the office, Graham unlocked the door and they climbed the stairs to the first floor.

'So this is where it all happens then?' asked Edward.

'You've got it!'

Edward threw his bunch of keys down on to his desk.

'When we first bought the Rectory I had imagined working from home. We've got enough space, after all. But Suzanne pointed out that it was more professional to operate from an office in town, so we looked round and found this place. The rent's not too bad and, to be honest, Suzanne was right. I've had no shortage of work since I've been here. I don't ever have to do much in the way of advertising.'

'So who, would you say, are your main clients? Residential or business?'

'A mixture really. I've done lots of extensions, new builds, conversions. Individual jobs. Then quite often I'll get approached by businesses to do plans and applications. More money in those of course, but the residential work is my bread and butter income.'

Edward scanned the office as his friend was talking. Graham was less tidy than him. He looked at the piles of plans and files stacked up on the desk, the used coffee cups piled up near the little sink in the corner and the calendar which was hanging at an angle from its hook on the wall and still showing last month's dates.

Graham knew instinctively what Edward was thinking and laughed.

'Alright Ed. Tell me if I've got this wrong – you're thinking no wonder Suzanne helped me look for this office. She didn't want me kicking around at home, making all this mess.'

Edward laughed too. He and Graham knew each other so well.

'Come on Mr Neat-And-Tidy. Bugger all this talking about work stuff. I'll take you for a quick walk round the rest of the town and then we'll get over to The White Hart for a pint.'

20

A few days later the Greenacre family returned to Humberside. During the return journey, Molly's mood was sombre and reflective. She had noticed a decline in her father's physical health which was troubling her, even though he had been bright, talkative and very appreciative of their visit.

He had taken Edward for a tour of the garden, pointing out all the new shoots and germinating seeds which showed so much promise for the forthcoming summer. It was good for her Dad to share time with Edward. They were such good friends.

Lizzie and Becky sat quietly in the back of the car, trying to fix their gaze on the horizon, as instructed, so as not to feel travel sick. Every so often they would forget, look down at the magazines Suzanne had given them as they left, argue about which ones they each wanted, and begin to feel queasy.

'Stop it. For heaven's sake. You can decide whose is whose and read those when you get home. Just be quiet. Your Dad needs to concentrate. And if you look down you're bound to feel sick.'

They would have to revert to looking out of the windows again and watch the verdant green countryside roll by. The green lushness made way for the familiar drab grey as they got closer to home.

All the way back Edward drove steadily and safely, but for the greater part of the journey he was thinking about the similarities, and the differences, of his career and Graham's.

Graham was his own boss, confidently making decisions about projects, building rapport with customers, sitting at a drawing board in his messy but bright office to produce beautifully detailed plans, and intelligently pricing jobs to ensure he was properly rewarded for his efforts. He didn't have unproductive or ill-mannered colleagues to deal with or have to carry out his work within the confines of restricting bureaucracy.

Okay, so he did have to deal with the planning department of the local authority when seeking permission on behalf of his clients for his projects, but Edward could imagine that Graham, with his technical expertise and effortlessly charming and confident manner, handled that with ease.

21

Molly thought it was high time that she made contact with friends they had left behind on the south coast when they moved to South Humberside two months and six days earlier. She had the morning to herself. Edward was at work, the girls were at school and the housework was up to date. She opened the bureau, took out a pad of Basildon Bond writing paper, a Parker ballpoint pen and her worn leather bound address book, then sat down at the dining room table. She would work methodically through the address book from A to Z, updating everyone with news of their eventful life in this bewildering town she was now forced to call home.

A – Shirley and Dennis Atkins.

'Dear Dennis and Shirley.

I do hope this finds you both well. It is just over two months since we left Winchester Road and relocated to South Humberside, but I must admit, it seems an awful lot longer! Edward's job is going very well. He has taken on a lot of responsibility, but seems to be thriving on that. The girls are at local schools and are both doing very well. Fortunately we live near enough for them to be able to walk to school – it usually takes them around 25 minutes. Lizzie and Becky have made some nice friends and both seem very happy in their new surroundings. Our house is finally getting organised although it has taken a while to get it straight as it is quite a bit smaller than our old one. We have had to be quite ruthless with our belongings and had to dispose of some items that we simply didn't have room for.

I do miss the crowd at WI. I haven't joined a group here yet as I have been so busy trying to sort out this house. Even now we still don't have all the boxes unpacked! How is everyone there? I imagine Mary is still as organised as ever, with her fundraising, cake-baking and strident rendition of 'Jerusalem'! I really must get round to joining the local group. They meet on a Wednesday evening, I think. And what about St Peter's? I gather you have a new vicar. It was a shame to see Walter depart, but I don't blame him for moving on to bigger and better things. He is a lovely man with a lot to offer any congregation. His Sunday communion services were such a pleasure to attend and I really do miss them. Again, Edward and I must get round to finding a local church we can attend. I am ashamed to admit that we have not yet done that!

Did you have any holidays over Easter? We went to Norfolk for a few days to stay with our friends Graham and Suzanne and to catch up with my parents. Graham and Suzanne live in a huge old rectory which they have done up and we thoroughly enjoyed spending time there. The coast is only about twenty minutes' drive from their house, so they took us there. It really was lovely. The smell of the sea breeze was a welcome antidote to the terrible smell of the steelworks we are forced to live with here. Admittedly we don't smell them every day. It depends which way the wind is blowing. If it's coming in from a westerly direction, we certainly know about it!

I have been thinking about Dennis' mother and wondering how she has been lately. I know that when we last spoke, she was in hospital. I hope that she made a good recovery and is now back at home. My mother was also unwell recently with a nasty chest infection but, thankfully, seems to be getting over the worst of it now. Dad is plodding along and cheerful despite his constant ill health. It's difficult living such a long way away and being unable to help. Ed's mother is her usual robust self. So no concerns there.

I will say goodbye for now. I hope that maybe sometime next year we can get down to see you both.

All the best.

Molly.'

And so the letter writing continued. She had considered including some information about the missing nine year old schoolgirl. It was all over the local news. Gone missing in this town while walking to school by herself. But that was only yesterday. Molly was sure she would be found safe and well, very soon hopefully, and by the time the recipients had received her letter that little girl would be safely back at home. Officer Fransham and Officer Melton would help see to that. They would have more on their plates than dealing with Shouty-Boy's older flower-flinging brother today. The little girl would be home, safe and sound and then it wouldn't be news anymore.

Molly worked her way, as intended, through her address book to the W's; the last three letters of the alphabet were a friendship wilderness. Each letter addressed to the couple, with the exception of one. 'Dear Peter and Diana' Molly had written, before ripping the paper from its pad, screwing it tightly into a ball and hurling it into the waste paper basket.

'Dear Diana. I hope this finds you well. It is just over two months since we left Winchester Road …'

It is two months and six days to be precise, thought Molly. Two months and one week since I was sitting on a bench with salt spray clinging in tiny, sparkling droplets to the wool fibres of my coat, listening to the seagulls, the waves breaking on the beach and the number 36 bus rattling along the road.

22

The following day there was still no good news concerning the missing nine-year-old, but the Greenacre girls, like hundreds of others this morning in this town, would have to get ready and walk to school.

'Come on girls. Time's getting on you know. Have you got everything you need for today? Homework in your bags?'

Lizzie and Becky responded to their mother's enquiry and confirmed that they did have everything they needed in their schoolbags.

'Well let's get downstairs then and have breakfast. I've done some porridge. I know it's May, but it's quite cold today,' Molly said, leading the way down to the kitchen. As she reached the bottom of the stairs and turned into the hallway Molly heard unfamiliar noises coming from outside at the front of the house. She glanced over into the sitting room and was confused to see a badly defaced window. Indecipherable red lettering covered most of the large picture window. Edward was the other side of the window with a bucket of steaming hot water and a scrubbing brush.

'What's going on, Ed?' called an apprehensive Molly from the front door which she had opened just wide enough to talk to her husband.

'I'm cleaning a few choice obscenities from our windows and walls. It seems that overnight some of our lovely neighbours have made their feelings perfectly clear. And some of them have also relieved themselves on our doorstep, so please, don't come out here Molly. Get back in the house.'

Sprawled across the front of house, across the large picture window and the brickwork, in what appeared to be red lipstick, were various permutations of the instruction to 'go away'.

'Girls; go into the kitchen and help yourselves to some breakfast. I'm just going to help Dad here and I'll be through in a few minutes.' She pulled her coat on, grabbed some cleaning cloths and another brush and went outside to join Edward, carefully avoiding the puddle of urine which had been left on their doorstep.

The sisters nervously did as instructed and spooned out hot porridge into the bowls Molly had left for them on the kitchen worktop. They stood in the kitchen, eating in silence and listening to the sound of scrubbing and their parents talking at low volume on the other side of the front door.

Edward and Molly worked together, cleaning the offensive messages from the brickwork and the windows and disinfecting the doorstep. Molly wondered if the offender was watching them as they cleaned. She couldn't tell from the writing whether a child or adult had committed this objectionable act, but surely children wouldn't be familiar with words like that, would they? She felt queasy, tearful and angry. The Greenacres were just an ordinary family; how, she wondered, could they have provoked such hostility. They had done nothing to warrant such unpleasant behaviour. Nothing like this would ever have happened at Winchester Road she thought. Certainly they had been the recipients of gifts left for them at the front of their house; eggs were regularly left by Frank who kept four brown hens in his back garden and last September Diana had left some flowers and a card for Molly on her birthday. Nice, friendly, generous gestures from congenial neighbours; not aggressive, repugnant demonstrations of hostility from repellent adversaries who might as well have scratched those obscenities into her aggrieved skin like an unsolicited tattoo. She scrubbed hard and angrily until the last remnants of the insolent tarnish were erased from the house then leaned the brush against the wall and went inside to see if her daughters had eaten their breakfast.

'I want to go home,' Lizzie said as her mother entered the kitchen.

'So do I,' echoed her sister.

'This IS home,' their mother replied. 'Now get your shoes and coats on and get off to school or you'll be late.'

23

'I've got some details of houses here,' Edward said to Molly a few days later, handing her a pile of papers.

'I think it would be an idea to spend the weekend looking at a few to see what we could get for our money. Like we said the other morning, we didn't intend to buy so soon, but after what happened last week now seems like the right time to move.'

Edward and Molly had agreed that they should move from the council house and buy a property in a nicer area to the south of the town.

The family went house hunting together. They looked at several different properties. Edward was drawn to an old cottage with a huge garden and crumbling plasterwork. Molly surprised herself by her ability to dissuade him from something which was, in her mind, completely unsuitable. Ceilings too low, location too rural, condition too poor. No, they really needed something they could just move into straightaway and situated in a reasonably convenient location for the school and Ed's work.

Becky liked the modern house with the bright pink bedroom but that was on a busy road and had no garage.

Just about a mile away from their final choice was a house Lizzie was convinced they should buy owing to the four leaf clover she found in the garden. That was a semi-detached house and the adjoining property looked very shabby and unloved. Molly couldn't bear the thought of living next door to a scruffy house again.

They finally decided on a modern detached house in a little cul-de-sac at the top of a hill. It had a garage, a reasonable sized garden, three bedrooms and more space downstairs than their current residence.

From the front of the house there were views across the town to the countryside beyond. Punctuating the otherwise pleasant view were the belching steelworks that could be clearly seen sending out huge plumes of acrid steam.

The location of the property was less convenient for Edward's commute and for the girls' school. They would have to catch a bus or ride their bicycles to their place of education. It was also further for Lizzie to travel to meet up with her friend, and two other girls that Lizzie had now befriended thanks to Helen. However, the Greenacre family were pleased that they could now look ahead to living in a nicer home.

24

'Ah! That's the post,' said Edward as he heard the letterbox clatter. 'Let's hope there's a letter from the solicitors.'

Edward had been drying up the breakfast crockery but now he put down the tea towel and collected the mail from the front door mat.

'Yes, it's here Molly. It should confirm the contract exchange and our move date.'

He put the other envelopes down on the worktop and opened the letter he had been eagerly awaiting.

'Good news?' asked Molly.

'July the twentieth. All arranged. We'll be in just as the school term finishes which is just what we wanted! You know, we were so lucky to find a house which was already empty. It's made the process so much more speedy.'

'Thank goodness,' said Molly. 'Our new home. It's happening!'

'It says here we will have to call into the solicitors to sign some more paperwork so I'll sort that out as soon as I can.

'July the twentieth. How far away is that?' Molly flicked through the calendar hanging on the kitchen wall. 'It's not long, Ed.'

'Well let's get packing!'

Despite it being only three months since they had last packed and unpacked their belongings, Edward was keen to get started on the arrangements for another move. Molly too was happy that they could focus on being in a nicer environment and she began to imagine that first summer in the garden. Perhaps a bit late in the season for much to happen this year but next she would be able to grow some vegetables and would enjoy the ritual of preparing delicious meals for her family with her home grown produce. The family would be able to sit round a fully extended table to eat or even eat outside as there was a large crazy paving patio at the back of the house.

Lizzie and Becky had never before been so relieved to see the end of term when their respective schools closed their doors for the summer holiday. Each of them brought home a school report.

Molly opened Becky's first and read the Headmaster's summary at the bottom of the page.

'Although Rebecca has only been with our school for a few weeks, she has proven herself to be a diligent and popular member of the class. She has shown particular aptitude in English and has achieved high marks for both reading and creative writing. We hope she can continue to do well in her studies when she moves up to Eastfield Comprehensive.'

Feeling relieved, Molly folded the report back up, put it to one side and turned to Lizzie's report.

'ENGLISH – Elizabeth's grasp of the subjects being studied in English is excellent but she needs to demonstrate this more effectively by speaking up in class. Her handwriting is excellent and all homework has been submitted on time.

'MATHEMATICS – Elizabeth is doing very well in Maths and if she continues to do well we will be working towards moving her up to a higher stream in the Autumn Term. She achieved eighty nine per cent overall in her end of year examinations which places her in the top quarter of the class. A good achievement considering she joined us part way through the academic year.

'ART – Elizabeth has shown promise throughout the term and has been experimenting with different mediums to produce some well observed work.'

'GERMAN – Despite not having studied this subject at her previous school, Elizabeth has shown a natural ability for the language. She now needs to concentrate on finding confidence to speak aloud in class.'

Molly would show Edward the reports tomorrow evening after they had got to their new house.

25

'Much left up there, Ed?' called Molly through the open roof hatch.

'Nearly done. If I pass this box to you can you take it and put it with the others on the landing?' Edward was standing with his feet carefully on the rafters and a large cardboard box in his hands.

'It's not heavy – just a bit bulky.'

'Okay Ed, pass them down.' Molly stood on the second rung of the step ladder, stretched up and took the first box from Edward who was now leaning precariously out of the hatch. The box had been labelled 'Photos and Colour Slides – 1969/1972'. It had been written in Edward's neat handwriting four months earlier. Molly took the box and placed them with the others – the heavier boxes that Edward had already brought down without her assistance. They were identified as 'Guide Books and Maps, Wedgwood, and 'Vases' and Molly was hopeful that at the new house she would have sufficient space to display her much loved Wedgwood collection. The blue items pleased her most, although she did have several green pieces too. Her favourite item was the little blue trinket box, adorned with the image of a Greek God and a ring of oak leaves around the outside of the lid. In it she kept all the tiny little beautifully hand-written notes that Edward had given to her when they first fell in love. She would keep them forever, and here they were again, being brought out of a cold, dark space into the daylight once more, preserved and protected by Asclepius.

'Can I take these now?' asked the driver of the removal van as he reached the top of the stairs.

'Yes, of course,' said Molly. 'Please be careful with the box on the end.'

'Don't worry, Mrs Greenwood. I may look a bit rough round the edges but I know that Wedgwood will break if it's handled badly.'

The man gave a little chuckle. 'Do I have to be careful with the one marked 'Vases' too?'

Molly laughed. 'If it's not too much trouble.'

Edward was now descending the step ladder and reaching up to pull the loft hatch back into position. He had one small cloth bag which he had hung from his right forearm.

'What's in here?' he asked Molly as he stepped back down on to the landing and peered inside the bag.

'Looks like a scarf. Is it silk? I've never seen you wear this Molly.'

'No well. It doesn't really go with anything,' said Molly, grabbing the bag swiftly from Edward and turning to go down the stairs.

Edward checked all three bedrooms and the bathroom for the final time. All empty. Thank goodness. He couldn't wait to get going. Downstairs he found Molly checking the understairs cupboard and with dustpan and brush in hand.

'Can you stick this in the car please,' she asked Ed. 'I just need to nip across to the post box and post these change of address cards.'

'You are organised,' Ed laughed 'Anyone would think you're keen to get away from here!'

'I'll be back in two ticks,' called Molly as she opened the back door. 'I've checked all the rooms downstairs now. Nothing left. We're ready to go.'

Molly walked quickly across to the post box up on the main road. She had in her hand forty six change of address cards and one special letter. She pushed them through the narrow opening and ran back to the car where her husband and daughters were waiting, and via number 83 who were busy adjusting their curtains.

26

The first week in their new home had lifted the Greenacre's collective spirits. Molly was busy doing most of the organising and unpacking as Edward wasn't able to get any time off work, but the girls had broken up from school and were helping Molly as best a thirteen and eleven year old could when they weren't arguing and annoying her.

The weather was kind to them. It was warm and sunny - Molly was hoping that would continue so that she could start working on the garden. The house had to be her priority at the moment, though.

There was just one reception room but it ran the full length of the house with windows at each end. It was light and spacious with plenty of space for their dining table at the far end of the room. Molly positioned it so that they would be able to look out over the garden while they ate.

The matching wall unit had been placed to the right hand side of the table and Molly enjoyed unpacking the best china and glasses and displaying them attractively on the shelves. The Wedgwood was allocated a large shelf all of its own.

Once the downstairs was reasonably straight, Molly moved on to the bedrooms, pushing the girls beds around until she felt they were it the best positions and hanging their clothes in the built in wardrobes.

By the end of the fifth day, the essential organisation was done and the rest could be done as time allowed. On his return from work each day, Edward was impressed with Molly's successive achievements and he would stand in the kitchen as she prepared the evening meal listening to her recap on the day's activities and then telling her about his own.

The back garden faced west and each day since they moved in had been filled with evening sunshine. On that fifth evening, while the potatoes were cooking, Molly and Edward went outside and sat on the patio with a glass of Chianti each.

'Cheers' said Edward as he chinked his wine glass against Molly's.

'Cheers,' she replied.

The couple sat silently for several minutes. Edward relaxing into the post-work warm glow of evening sunshine and the effects of the Chianti and Molly surveying the garden and planning in her head how it would all look by the end of the summer.

I'm looking at that bit of the garden on the left and thinking that would be a good place to grow some veg.' Molly gestured with her free hand towards the piece of garden she had in mind. 'What do you think, Ed?'

'You're the gardener,' Ed replied. 'If you think that's the best spot, then put them there. Do you want me to get you a shed for your tools?'

'Well, they've just been shoved in the garage for now, but they would be best in a shed. Can we afford one?'

'Of course, we can,' said Ed, taking a large sip of wine. 'Where should I site it? At the far end near the fence?'

'Or backing on to the garage, tucked round the corner?' suggested Molly.

'Could do. Depends on how big a one you need. How big was the one at Winchester Road?'

'Eight foot by six. Oh, and that reminds me, talking of Winchester Road, Diana has invited Lizzie down to stay at the end of next week.'

'That will be nice. Did the invitation not extend to Becky though?'

'Well Judith is Lizzie's friend really, so what I was thinking was that I could take Lizzie down on the train and bring Siobhan back to stay here so that Becky's got some company. As long as her parents are agreeable to that.'

'It's a long old journey by train. Why don't I take you in the car?'

'Not necessary, Ed. Besides, you'll be at work. It will be so much easier for me to travel down one day with Lizzie and back with Siobhan on the following day.' Molly picked up her wine glass and took a much bigger mouthful of wine than she would normally have done.

'I'll ask at work tomorrow. I'm sure Mayhew can manage for one day without me. As long as he's not in one of his moods.'

'There's no need, Ed. It's all arranged. We're going down on the train on Friday week. I'll be back on Saturday.' Molly picked up her glass and went inside to strain the potatoes.

27

Molly was in the sitting room ironing her way through a large basket full of clean linen when she heard the doorbell ring. She glanced at the clock which read 10.20am. She was expecting someone to come round and measure up for a new carpet in Lizzie's bedroom, but they weren't due for at least another half hour. She carefully put down the iron and walked into the hallway.

'Hello,' said an unfamiliar man as Molly opened the front door. 'I'm Colin. I live at Number Three.' Colin was holding a small houseplant in a ceramic pot. 'I've bought you a moving-in gift.'

'How very kind of you,' said Molly. 'Come in please.'

Colin, a short and slightly overweight man with thick framed glasses and grey hair, probably in his 60's, Molly thought, accepted the invitation, wiped his feet on the doormat and closed the door behind him before following Molly through to the kitchen.

'I'm Molly,' she said. 'Lovely to meet you. And thank you so much for the plant,' she continued as Colin handed it over to her.

'You're welcome. I grew it myself from a cutting.'

'How lovely.'

'Plants and gardening are what keep me going. I've got a small greenhouse out the back. I'm going to try and grow a few vegetables from seed this year, once I have repaired the broken glass. It got damaged in those gales we had last winter. Gardening fills the time and filling the time is necessary when you're retired and live alone, or you'd go mad.'

'Yes, I'm sure,' said Molly politely.

'So how are you settling in? I saw the removal van turn up last week with all your stuff.'

'Well, there's a lot to do but we're getting it through it now. We've got it straight enough to realise we're going to enjoy living here, so that's good.'

'It's a good place to live. I can't say I enjoy it myself though I'm afraid.'

Molly wondered if she was meant to feel guilty and respond with a relevant question to her visitor's last statement. Fortunately, within a couple of seconds of Molly trying to formulate an appropriate but not too familiar answer, her visitor picked up his side of the conversation again.

'So where have you moved from? You sound like you've come from down South somewhere.'

Molly decided he didn't need to know about Greenacre's former residence for the last four months. 'Yes, that's right. My husband has taken on a job at the Council, so we've moved up here.'

'I've seen him drive off in the mornings,' Colin said. 'And you've got two daughters?'

'Yes, they'll be going to Eastfield Comprehensive. Off school for summer holidays at the moment and today they've gone into the town. Molly deliberately held back from mentioning the girls' names as she was beginning to feel that Colin was a bit too interested in knowing the finer details of their family life. It was too early on in this neighbourly relationship to be divulging a lot of information, houseplant gift or not. Colin must have spent a lot of time looking out from number three at their arrival and their subsequent movements in and out of the house over the last few days.

'I've lived in the close since these houses were built,' Colin said. 'Seen a few families come and go. I think there are only a handful of us who've been here from the start. Have you met the Wilsons at Number Seven?'

'No, we haven't had a chance yet, what with trying to unpack and the girls being off school.'

'Well, I would say Martin and Glenda are about your age and they've got a daughter too. They moved into the close as newly-weds same day as me, so I've seen them make changes to the house, have the baby – a young woman now of course - buy and sell several different cars (Martin likes his cars) and completely change the layout of the garden. They've recently put up a nice summerhouse in the back. Glenda's the gardener and she's transformed the place. Yes, I've seen it all happen at Number Seven.'

I bet you have, thought Molly, wondering if their own lives were going to be scrutinised in the same way.

'Then there's Mrs Barrett next door to them. She's getting on a bit now. 83 next week she is, but still looks after herself. I keep an eye on her, you know, when her daughter's not around. Do a bit of shopping for her, cut the front grass, that sort of thing.'

There were twenty three houses in Redridge Close. Molly hoped she wasn't going to get an intimate run through of the whole lot and was beginning to wonder how she could excuse herself from further briefings as the iron was still on and would be ticking away in the room next door as it heated up and cooled down again.

Colin was about to launch into the next instalment of his thrilling trip around Redridge Close, when the doorbell rang.

'Oh, excuse me Colin. I think that will be the carpet fitter.'

'I'll get going then. Leave you to it. Oh, and by the way, here's my telephone number. You are more than welcome to pop across and use the 'phone if there's an emergency of any kind.' Colin put down a scrappy piece of paper on the kitchen worktop.

Molly answered the front door, very grateful that the fitter had arrived earlier than scheduled. Colin stood back to allow him to pass him in the hallway, acknowledged him with a quick 'Hello Mate' and then made his way down the short driveway and back across the road to Number Three.

'Thanks again for the plant,' Molly called. 'And for the telephone number. I'll pass it on to my Mum if that's alright.' She closed the front door.

'I'm sorry to be a little earlier than arranged.'

'No, don't apologise. It's absolutely fine. Great timing, in fact.'

28

Dear James

Just a quick note as the carpet fitter took longer than expected and I need to get out, get this posted and back again before the wardrobe is delivered this afternoon. Arrangements are all organised now. I will meet you on Friday night – 5.40pm usual place.

Much love, as always,
Molly x

29

The next few days passed without incident. Molly kissed her husband goodbye as he left for work each morning and continued to deal with domestic chores around their new home. Lizzie regularly met up with Helen and the two other girls she had now befriended. Becky too spent time with friends she had met through junior school and who would also be moving up to the Comprehensive in September.

The first Friday in August was the day that had been arranged for Molly to take Lizzie down to stay with Judith. On the previous evening Lizzie said goodbye to Helen for a few days and packed a few clothes into a holdall that Molly had given her.

'Have you got everything you need Lizzie?' called Molly up the stairs. 'Toothbrush? Clean socks? A warm jacket in case the weather turns cooler?'

Lizzie ran back into the bathroom to grab her toothbrush and shoved it into her drawstring washbag which already contained everything else she might need.

'Yes. Coming down now.'

'We're all waiting for you. Hurry up. I DO NOT want to miss our train.'

Lizzie ran downstairs, grabbed her jacket which was hanging over the end of the bannisters and went outside to get in the car. Molly locked up the house and joined the others. It was still early in the morning as Edward was dropping his wife and eldest daughter at the station, then leaving Becky with a friend before going on to work. Despite the early hour, the resident at Number Three watched them depart from Redridge Close.

As Edward pulled out on to the main road and began the short journey to the station, Molly looked over her shoulder to address Becky in the rear seat. 'Daddy's going to pick you up from Sarah's after tea. You're staying for tea with Sarah, alright? Then tomorrow you'll be at home with Daddy and I am going to get back with Siobhan around 4 o'clock.' Molly turned back to talk to Ed.

'Can you collect us from the station at ten past four?'

'Yes, that's fine. Ten past four. Tomorrow. The station. Got it.' Ed was concentrating on manoeuvering the car round some vehicles which had been parked on the side of the road.

Molly turned back to Becky. 'We'll sort out the campbed and sleeping bag for Siobhan tomorrow when I'm back, so please try and keep your room tidy, won't you?'

Becky nodded. Lizzie looked out of the window. She was extremely happy that the arrangements had been made in such a way that she wouldn't have to have any contact with Becky's vicious little friend.

30

'Good morning Elsie,' said Edward as he walked into the Admin Office. 'Morning Mr Greenacre,' replied Elsie, smiling. 'You're here bright and early today.'

'Just dropped my wife and eldest daughter at the station and then youngest at a friend's house. Didn't take me as long as I was expecting. How are you, anyway? Looking forward to the weekend, no doubt.'

'Indeed. I'm off to the theatre tomorrow and out to lunch on Sunday.' Elsie leaned round to the shelves behind her desk and picked up a pile of papers.

'You have a full weekend then. Excellent.'

'Here's the work you asked me to type up for you. I've made two carbon copies as requested.'

Edward took the documents from Elsie and smiled. 'I can always rely on you, can't I? Thank you. I'll get these signed and then hand them back to you for posting later today with the attachments.'

Edward turned to leave and Elsie called after him. 'Mr Jameson's secretary, Jennifer, wants a word. She asked if you could call in to her office first thing.'

'Righteo,' replied Edward 'I'll head up there now.' The Admin Office door swung shut behind him.

Edward climbed two flights of stairs to his own office and put down his briefcase and the paperwork he had just collected from Elsie on his desk. No sign of Mayhew yet. On reflection, Ed thought, that's because it's still only ten to nine and Mayhew never got in before nine. In fact, on a Friday it's more likely to be ten past nine.

'Good Morning John,' Ed said as he heard the office door open and saw his dour colleague enter.

'Morning' replied miserable John Webster and without any further pleasantries he slumped down into his office chair and pulled out a pack of cigarettes from his jacket pocket.

Edward knew it would be pointless trying to engage him in further conversation so he turned around, caught the door as it was still swinging and made his way up to the top floor of the building.

Mr Jameson's office was at the far end of the corridor and Jennifer occupied a smaller adjoining space. Edward was curious about why Jennifer needed to speak to him, but there was only one way to find out. He knocked lightly on the door, even though it was ajar.

'Good morning Jennifer. How are you?' said Edward, poking his head around the door. Jennifer was at her desk feeding paper through the rollers of her typewriter.

'Come in Edward,' she said, smiling. 'Take a seat.'

Edward sat down in the seat opposite Jennifer and glanced through to Jameson's office. He noticed he wasn't in the office yet.

'Mr Jameson not here yet?' enquired Edward. It was a rhetorical question and somewhat stating the obvious.

'Off today,' replied Jennifer. 'Playing golf.'

'I see,' said Edward who was beginning to feel a little uncomfortable, although he didn't know why.

'Edward,' said Jennifer, looking at him straight in the eye and still smiling. 'I need to ask you a favour.'

'Glad to be of service,' said Edward, trying to sound confident.

'But you don't know what the favour is yet.'

'True, but ...'

'It's a personal matter really. Not related to work exactly.'

Edward was puzzled. He felt a little naïve and wasn't sure he wanted to be part of this dialogue.

'Charles Nicholson,' said Jennifer.

'Charles?' said Edward. 'What of him?'

'What do you know of his personal circumstances?'

'What do you mean exactly?'

'Well he's a bit of a dark horse, isn't he?'

'Erm ... I'm not sure ... Is he?'

'Do you know if he's married or has a girlfriend?'

'No. We haven't had those kind of conversations.' Edward felt even more uncomfortable now.

'Well try and find out for me, would you? Have a different kind of conversation,' laughed Jennifer. 'And there's one more favour.'

Edward's heart sank.

'Mr Jameson is celebrating a special birthday next month. We've had a collection for him.'

'Yes, I know. I dropped a couple of coins in the envelope.'

'We've got a fair amount. The collection has been round every office now. I have got the responsibility of buying something. I was thinking a nice tie pin and matching cuff-links. What do you think?'

Edward was now rather desperate to leave Jennifer's office. He didn't mind contributing to Jameson's birthday collection, but he didn't want to have to decide how it was spent. And he certainly did not want to have any hand in match-making with Nicholson.

'Tie pin and cuff-links. Good idea.' Edward got up ready to leave.

'So you'll come into town with me at lunchtime and help choose some then? I need a man who has some class and can choose wisely.'

He was caught off-guard. He couldn't think of an excuse quick enough, so he responded in a reluctant affirmative and went out into the corridor, regretting his inability, in this instance, to choose wisely.

31

Judith took Lizzie to revisit some old haunts. Today it would be the park. They strolled down Winchester Road, passing number 186 and Scratchbum Lane as they did so, crossed the main street at the traffic lights and continued on the park entrance near the river. The sun was high in a cloudless sky and it was creating dark, short shadows on the ground. Both girls were wearing the hot pants they had purchased in C & A the previous day. Diana had taken them into the city and they girls had been left to their own devices for an hour, with holiday money in hand.

Lizzie and Judith pushed open the metal entrance gate and strolled across to the roundabout. They each sat down on one of the eight wooden segments, Judith pushing off with her foot as they did so. The wood, heated by the mid-summer sun, felt delightfully warm against the backs of their legs. The roundabout began to travel slowly round and the girls watched as all the familiar sights passed their eyes: the strip of worn grass between the entrance gate and the play area, the metal fencing which ran along the edge of the park with the river beyond, a row of tall evergreen trees at the back of the park which bordered Church Lane, the railway station, the row of shops including the bakers with the friendly baker, and back around to the worn grass strip. The roundabout took five revolutions, gradually slowing to a stop while the girls chatted effortlessly with each other. Lizzie stepped off and re-started the roundabout but there was no pause in their easy conversation.

'Shall we go over and see if Susan is at home?' Judith suggested, after several minutes had gone by and when it was apparent a group of younger children were becoming impatient with waiting for their turn to use the roundabout.

'She probably will be,' replied Lizzie stepping down, the backs of her legs marked with red stripes from the wooden slats.

Susan was a friend from Guides and school and was the daughter of the local vicar. She lived in the vicarage only a short distance away. Judith and Lizzie walked back along the threadbare grass, out of the metal gate, and headed left down the street towards Church Lane at the end. They ambled slowly, the sunlight glinting off the shallow river on one side of them as it gurgled and splashed across the lichen covered stones. On their right hand side was a row of large detached houses; a mixture of grand double fronted villas, flint and brick walls marking their boundaries, interspersed with their modern counterparts. They all sat on orderly plots of land. The trees in the front gardens of the older properties were large and stately whilst those in the newer houses were still maturing but equally vigorous at this stage in the season. Butterflies and bees were flitting and humming around the colourful flowers, and chittering birds were darting backwards and forwards from the ground to the branches overhead, grabbing seeds or insects which were in abundance.

Judith and Lizzie turned the corner at the end of the road, walked over the stone bridge which crossed the river, and on to the vicarage.

Judith gave two knocks of the brass door knocker. Immediately there was enthusiastic barking coming from behind the large oak door. It was soon opened by Susan's mother who gave the girls a bright 'Hello!' Two Golden Retrievers, who had now stopped barking, came rushing out and began excitedly circling the visitors, wiggling their rear ends and looking for affection.

'Come on boys,' said Susan's mother gently to the dogs. 'Inside please.'

Lizzie and Judith, walked into the dark cool hallway, patting the dogs on the head as they did so. The boys ambled off back to the huge kitchen and flopped back down on to their beds, emitting contented little canine grumbling noises as they did so.

'It's so lovely to see you again, Lizzie. Staying down here with Judith for a few days?'

'Yes,' nodded Lizzie, a little meek and suddenly feeling shy as she sensed Susan's mother's genuine affection for her.'

Susan was upstairs, at the far end of the large vicarage but had heard the commotion below and was on her way along the landing. She smiled happily as she rounded the top of the wide staircase and could see her friends standing below. It was only two weeks into the summer holidays but she was bored already. Judith and Lizzie would be a welcome diversion for the rest of the day.

'Susan, can I hear your record player still running upstairs?' asked her mother who could easily detect 'Metal Guru' bouncing off the lilac wallpapered walls in her daughter's bedroom.

'It's okay Mum, I'll turn it off when we go out,' said Susan, skidding round on her heels and gesturing to her friends to join her. 'Come upstairs while I get changed.'

Judith and Lizzie ran upstairs and followed Susan along the landing, entering the end room where Marc Bolan was loudly insistent with his enquiry regarding the identity of the man without the telephone.

32

Molly was out in the garden trimming the grass round the edge of the newly extended flower bed. Today was a beautiful summer day. The breeze was blowing the steelworks stench in the opposite direction so Molly had all the windows open to air the whole house. She was trying to decide what plants she would put in the new bed - Antirrhinums, Lavender and Marigolds at the front and maybe Hollyhocks at the rear - but was distracted by the noise of Siobhan and Becky arguing in the bedroom. It sounded as though Siobhan was being bossy again and Molly knew, that for the third time this week, she would have to down tools and go and sort out a squabble. Becky had been reduced to tears by the last quarrel and Molly was beginning to resent having to look after Siobhan for a whole week if she was going to continue to behave in this way. Siobhan had also been fussy at mealtimes, picking through Molly's delicious home cooked food and complaining about what she didn't like. Roll on Saturday, now only two days away, when Edward would drive them 120 miles southward to the half way point, meet Diana, and swap Siobhan for Lizzie. Diana had kindly offered to take Siobhan back to her parents as she was coming up anyway to bring Lizzie part of the way home. Molly was sure, that at Diana's house, Lizzie would be a more respectful guest than Siobhan had been here. Elizabeth and Rebecca Greenacre had been raised to be polite, especially in someone else's home. When it was clear the argument wasn't going to sort itself out, Molly angrily threw down the edging shears, kicked her gardening shoes off at the back door and went upstairs to resolve matters.

Although she managed to temporarily restore peace on the first floor of 11 Redridge Close and resume her work in the garden for a while, Molly was glad when Edward returned home from work.

'Goodness! You have been busy. Look at this, exclaimed Edward who had wandered outside on to the patio when he realised his wife wasn't at her usual spot in the kitchen at this time of day.

'Do you like it? I was thinking Snapdragons at the front just here.' Molly gestured with the garden fork. 'I know you like them.'

Edward walked across the lawn to his wife and kissed her tenderly on the cheek. She looks radiant and content, Edward thought, standing back to admire her horticultural handiwork once more. Molly's hair was held back with a headband but several strands had escaped and were blowing across her face. She pushed them away with the back of a muddy hand and left a thin streak of soil on her forehead.

'And Sunflowers? At the back?' Molly suggested. 'With some Hollyhocks too, of course.'

'We're only having Sunflowers if you promise me they'll be as tall as those we grew at Winchester Road,' laughed Edward.

'They were absolute monsters, weren't they? And the ones at Hambleton Cottage. I think they were even bigger.'

'Can you remember when Lizzie found out that parrots liked sunflower seeds, and sent one of the flower heads into Blue Peter?' Ed asked.

'She was so proud of her badge.' Molly recalled, smiling.

'That poor parrot. He died not long after that.'

33

Susan changed her clothes and made a half-hearted attempt at tidying her room. She chatted to her friends as she did so, occasionally having to raise her voice so that she could be heard above the louder bits of musical offerings from T Rex, Wizzard and Stevie Wonder. Back downstairs in the huge but homely kitchen, the Vicar's wife was preparing sandwiches, cake and squash for her daughter and her guests. The three girls came downstairs, devoured their lunch then set off back towards the park. Lizzie and Judith politely expressed their thanks as they left and patted the dogs on the head once more.

The day was now at its hottest and the girls walked under the shade of the trees along the river, stopping to sit on the shallow grassy bank for a while, flinging their sandals to one side and dangling their feet in the cool, clear water.

'What's your new school like Lizzie?' asked Susan, idly poking the grass with a stick she'd picked up from the bank.

Lizzie lay back on the grass and looked up at the dancing bright green leaves of the tree above them. She closed her eyes. Flecks of sunlight skipped across her face and torso.

'It's horrible. Our English teacher's alright and I don't mind Art either. But the rest is horrible.' Her answer required no response or sympathy from Susan. It was just a statement of the facts as Lizzie saw them.

'Mr Campbell has left,' said Susan.

'Yes,' confirmed Judith. 'Silly old codger.'

'Why?' enquired Lizzie, wondering why her former history teacher might have left the job he'd held since the Roman Invasion. About which he was constantly talking.

'Got too old for teaching.'

'Excuse me girls,' said a voice from the road above the bank. 'Sorry to interrupt your chat.'

Lizzie sat upright and looked round, shielding her eyes from the sun with her right hand. She saw a man, aged about the same age as her Dad, but much shorter, with a camera hanging from a strap over his shoulder. He was wearing a pale green shirt with the sleeves rolled up and trousers which were too long.

'I work for the Gazette. Doing a feature on the local area. Would you mind if I took your photo?'

He walked down the bank, and took the camera from his shoulder.

'If you could just turn round a little towards me, but don't look at the camera - look down into the river just like you were doing.'

Judith, Lizzie and Susan were rather excited about having their picture in the local paper so did as requested and heard several clicks of the shutter.

'That's it. Thank you.'

The girls turned back to face the man. His flies were undone and he was exposing himself.

It took less than a second for him to ascertain that each of the three girls had witnessed his revelation. He then tidied himself up, flung the camera back over his shoulder and ran up the bank out of sight.

34

Edward descended the two flights of stairs to the Admin Office. Following a busy day yesterday, he had in his hands a large pile of handwritten notes and forms which needed typing up. Elsie would handle them with her usual efficiency he thought. He flicked though them as he walked through the door, ensuring they were all in the correct order and had been clearly marked with the number of carbon copies required. It was now just over four months since he started this job. He felt like he was in the swing of it and could see that he was performing a really vital part of the social housing regeneration process. He enjoyed getting out of the office and meeting tenants, especially those who were initially hesitant about having to move out of their home while it was being renovated. Winning those type of tenants round was a challenge but very satisfying when it all came right. It gave Edward a huge sense of achievement. Liaising with the contractors was another part of the job in which he had really taken pleasure. They all respected him and he came to look forward to the meetings he held with them. They were a satisfying mix of professionalism and repartee. Edward tried hard to put the downsides of his work to one side. The unpredictability of Mayhew's mood and the surliness of some of the others in his office he found unsettling. He took it personally and didn't know why they behaved like that towards him. He didn't deserve it and it was beginning to knock his usual unwavering positive attitude. When he got home yesterday evening he had tried to talk to Molly about it but she was too wrapped up in how terrible her day had been looking after someone else's objectionable child. Her lack of sympathy for him last night had taken him by surprise and upset him much more than he thought it would. He had come to rely on Molly for support but last night it was all about Siobhan and her terrible manners. Surely an eleven year old child was easier to deal with, no matter how badly behaved, than several ill-natured adults with whom you were forced to share five days out of seven? Thank goodness tomorrow was Saturday and they could return the offensive child to her parents via Diana. Molly would be relieved of her duties and would be back to her usual supportive self.

As he entered the Admin Office Edward noticed that Elsie was not at her desk.

'You looking for Elsie?' A voice came from behind him which he instantly recognised.

Edward turned around to see Jennifer had followed him in.

'Yes,' said Edward. 'More typing.' He lifted up the pile of paperwork slightly to demonstrate his point.' At this point he was smiling weakly and willing Elsie to appear and save him.

'She's off today. I'll do your typing for you if you like.' Jennifer was looking straight at Edward with her striking hazel eyes.

'There's no need. None of it is especially urgent. I'll see Elsie on Monday with it.'

'Come on, Edward. Let me help you. It would be my pleasure.'

'No. Really. It's not necessary. Besides I expect you have enough of Mr Jameson's work to be getting on with.'

'I insist, Ed' said Jennifer and took the files from him, brushing her hand against his as she did so. 'I'll have them all finished by 4pm. Come up and get them then.'

35

'Do you think we should tell our Mums or Dads?' asked Judith, giggling nervously.

'God, no!' said Susan. 'Mine would go bonkers. In any case it would be so embarrassing.'

'I agree,' said Lizzie. 'SO embarrassing.'

'Let's just pretend it didn't happen then,' suggested Susan. 'I don't think we'll get our picture on the front of the Gazette anyway.' She giggled too and stood up. 'Come on. Let's walk over to the shops and get an ice lolly.'

By the time the girls reached the top of the bank the man had disappeared and they were able to walk to the main road without any further incident. They crossed the road and went into the newsagents where they each purchased a lolly, carefully counting out the required number of coins and placing them on the wooden counter top. Each girl threw their respective wrapper into the bin outside the shop and strolled along the wide pavement while they ate them. The heat of the sun made was making them melt so they deftly licked the sticky, brightly coloured drips before they ran down their hands.

'I've got some money left. I'm going to get my Mum a birthday present,' said Susan, tossing the lolly stick into another bin and entering the Chemists. 'You coming?'

Lizzie bit the last bit of lolly off her stick, hurled it at the bin and followed Susan and Judith in. The shop smelled of a delicious concoction of lavender, sandlewood and musk.

They wandered up the perfume aisle, considering Tweed at first, but then Judith thought Aqua Manda might smell nicer. It was a bit more expensive though. But the box was far prettier.

'What about this?' asked Lizzie, holding up a bottle of 4711.

'Reminds me of my Nanna. No thanks,' laughed Susan.

The girls looked at all possibilities, taking price, scent, attractiveness of the box and ease of wrapping all into consideration. In the end, Susan's choice was determined by price alone as she hadn't got much money left. Judith and Susan went up to the till at the back of the shop to pay and joined a small queue. Lizzie walked round to the other aisle. There were rows of hairbrushes hanging neatly from a row of hooks, a bit further along was the soap and opposite the make-up. A little section of each of the different brands. Lizzie, like her father, had an appreciation of good aesthetics. She was intoxicated by the displays and rows of different colours, sizes and shapes of the products and how they made for one overall attractive picture. Her mother wouldn't let her wear make-up but she would be fourteen soon and surely that meant she would be eligible to wear it? The models on the pictures at the top of the display smiled out at Lizzie with their shiny lips and mauve painted eyelids, defined by smoky kohl. She picked up a lipstick and rolled it satisfyingly round in her hand, before replacing it and swapping it for a little tray which contained four eye-shadows. The palette contained sparkly grey at one end, and sparkly pink at the other. The two colours in the middle were mauve and blue. Lizzie imagined herself wearing the mauve, like the model in the photograph right above her. It was such a pretty colour. Susan had now paid for the perfume and was walking towards Lizzie with Judith following on behind.

'Got it!' said Susan, waving a little paper bag which contained her purchase and passing Lizzie in the aisle. 'Shall we go to the park now?'

Lizzie quickly looked around. No one was watching. Her friends were already out on the pavement. She slipped the eye-shadow tray into the pocket of her hot pants and followed her friends out on to the street.

36

Diana arrived at the service station half an hour before the time she had arranged to meet Edward. It had been an easy journey. She found a space, drove in forwards and pulled on the handbrake. In the rear view mirror she could see her daughter and Lizzie. The past week had been lovely and Diana was pleased that Judith and her friend had got on so well for the entire time. As an only child, Judith was sometimes very clingy with her mother who often felt guilty about not providing her with a sibling. There was Peter to thank for that. Diana firmly believed that having friends was wonderful, but she considered relationships with siblings went much deeper than just companionship. She had two sisters of her own and they shared a strong bond. It was a terrible shame that Judith's best friend had moved so far away, Diana thought, but having Lizzie to stay this week had been beneficial for all concerned.

'Your Dad will be here soon, Lizzie,' said Diana, over her shoulder.

Lizzie smiled a forced smile. Her thoughts on being reunited with her parents and Becky back in Stinksville could be described as ambivalent at best. She had thoroughly enjoyed the last week. Well, most of it anyway.

'Shall we get out and walk along the bank? Be good to get some air, even if it is on the side of a busy road.' Diana got out of the car and her passengers put down their magazines and joined her on the path which ran between the rows of vehicles.

The grassy bank along which they walked was lined with trees. There was a sharp drop behind the trees leading down to the main road and, being the middle of the holiday season, it was busy with the constant hum of traffic. The trees were relatively young so they afforded only a little shade, but it felt good to be out of the car and being mobile again. The girls walked ahead of Diana. She watched them chatting easily and laughing. They were both tall and slim, their lithe limbs tanned from the plentiful sunshine of the last few weeks. She suddenly felt a pang of sadness and realised that she was missing Molly. They too had enjoyed an easy friendship, with lots in common and a shared love of gardening, the coast and family. She regretted not having spent more time with Molly and Edward as a couple, but again, that was more Peter's decision than hers. Those sort of regrets are pointless though, she thought. Nothing can be changed now. Edward had convinced Molly that moving away was a good thing to do and they did it. Unlikely they'll ever return, and even if they did, would it be the same? I must snap out of this melancholy mood, thought Diana. The girls will pick up on it. Edward will be here soon too. Diana brushed away an unwelcome tear and was grateful that the girls didn't notice.

She looked at her watch. Edward wasn't the kind of man to be late, so they should turn around and walk back to the car.

'Judith. Lizzie. Let's turn around now,' Diana called.

The two friends looked round and saw Diana beckoning to them. Slowly they followed her back along the grassy bank and down to the car. Within a few minutes they saw Edward's car arrive at the entrance to the car park and he turned into a space just two rows away from Diana.

'Edward,' called Diana. 'How lovely to see you. How are you?'

'I'm well. Very well in fact,' replied Edward as he got out of his car and held his hand out to shake Diana's. 'Hello Lizzie. Good week?'

Lizzie nodded.

'Thank you so much for agreeing to meet here, Diana. And thanks too for looking after Elizabeth all week. I hope she's behaved herself and been a good guest.'

'Of course. It's been a pleasure. Judith has really enjoyed the company. I've hardly seen them actually. They've been out and about meeting up with friends, shopping, and so on. We've been so fortunate with the weather so they've not been short of things to do.'

'Wonderful,' replied Edward. 'Shall we go in and get a cup of tea or are you wanting to get straight back?'

'We'll get going if you don't mind Edward. Siobhan's mother needs her back by teatime.'

Siobhan had already got out of Edward's car and was standing at the back, drawing a picture of a cat with her finger in the dust which had accumulated on the rear window.

'Fair enough. I think we will go in. I'm parched. Do you want a drink Lizzie?'

Lizzie nodded.

'Well, thanks once again Diana,' said Edward taking Lizzie's bag which Diana had just removed from the boot of her car and swapping it for Siobhan's. 'Safe journey. Oh, and Molly sends her regards. Says she'll write next week.'

'Thanks Ed,' said Diana, opening the rear door for Judith and Siobhan.

'Come on girls. In you get. We'll get going now.'

Judith and Siobhan got into the car and Diana closed the boot lid and walked round to the driver door.

'Bye Ed.'

Diana reversed out of her space and began the journey southwards, back home.

Once out on the main road and after fifteen minutes of silence from the back seat, Diana thought she should engage her youngest passenger in conversation.

'So, Siobhan. How's your week been? Good?' Diana was looking in her rear view mirror and could see there was a mere shrug in response.

'Was it nice to see Rebecca again?'

Still no verbal reply. Siobhan was looking out of the window.

'What did you do? Did you go anywhere nice?'

Siobhan clearly did not want to converse so Diana ignored the sullenness and concentrated on getting her back home to her parents, safely, but as swiftly as she could.

Meanwhile Edward was suitably refreshed and was walking across the car park with Lizzie towards his car.

'We'll be back home by about four, I reckon Lizzie.'

They got into the car. Edward started the engine then put the car into reverse gear. He checked his rear view mirror and, even though it was a back to front image, could see, written in the dust on the window 'cat piss' and an arrow pointing towards a crudely drawn image of a cat's bottom.

37

Back in the council offices two days later, Edward was busy organising the schedule for the next batch of houses he and Mayhew were due to inspect. Edward's colleague was evading any contribution to this process and kept finding reasons to leave the office so that he didn't have to be involved. It seemed to Edward that Mayhew was becoming less compliant as each week passed with seemingly no guilt attached to his behaviour or how it was impacting on balancing the workload. Edward didn't complain or reveal his concern – he just worked twice as hard to get through all the necessary arrangements and ensure the job would be carried out to Jameson's full satisfaction. Today though he would have to take a break himself to go out at lunchtime and pick up some curtain hooks from Woolworths. Molly was making new curtains for their bedroom with some colourful fabric she had purchased at the market last week but needed more hooks. It would be a good excuse to get away from his desk for a while.

At 1pm Edward shuffled his papers into a neat pile, took his jacket from the back of his chair and tucked his pen into the inside pocket. He would need a jacket today. The weather was grey and much cooler of late. Glancing out of the window on the way to the swing doors which led out to the landing he noticed Jennifer crossing the carpark towards the building. A quick calculation indicated to Edward that he should find something to do for the next three minutes to avoid crossing on the stairs. He turned around and went to study a map on the wall which showed all the areas being currently worked on and those yet to do. The completed areas had been neatly cross hatched in red pen. Looking at it, Edward was struck by how much there still was left to do.

'Hello Edward.'

Edward turned around and saw Jennifer standing behind him. He hadn't heard the swing doors open so was startled to suddenly find her in the office and so uncomfortably close to him.

'I need a favour Edward,' said Jennifer, smiling and looking straight at him while smoothing several strands of glossy light brown hair over her shoulder.

Oh God. Not another one, thought Edward.

'Of course. My pleasure,' said Edward, polite and gentlemanly as ever, but secretly dreading the unknown favour had just agreed to.

'My car is making the most terrible noise. I'm sure you're good with your hands. Would you mind taking a look for me?'

'I'm just off out to pick up something for my wife. Won't be too long I shouldn't think. I need to get to Woolworths to get some curtain hooks. My wife's making some curtains for ... erm ... anyway, I will be just a short while. Mayhew and I have a deadline to meet with some paperwork when I get back, so it will be middle of the afternoon before I can get down there and see what's up. Is it parked on the carpark?'

Edward realised that his feeling of awkwardness was causing him to gabble.

'Far side, second row in, near the exit. Here's my keys.' Jennifer dangled the car keys by a shiny fob with her neatly manicured hand.

'Thank you,' mumbled Edward and accepted the bunch of keys with trepidation. The metal felt uncomfortably warm in his hands. 'I'll just run this errand for my wife and come up and see you in your office later.'

Edward was thankful that the only other person in the office at the time was on the telephone so wouldn't have witnessed this conversation.

'I'm so grateful to you Edward,' said Jennifer as she crossed the office to leave. She pushed open the swing doors, looking over her shoulder at Edward as she did so.

'See you later.'

Edward left the offices and crossed the carpark towards the high street, glancing over to the second row in as he made his way out of the exit. He made a mental note of the space in which the reportedly noisy blue Hillman Imp was parked and he felt an alarming sinking feeling in his stomach. He tried hard to push the feeling to one side and focus instead on the job in hand. Woolworths. Curtain hooks. Should find them on the first floor. In bags of twenty. Get two bags. Molly had nearly finished the curtains and was counting on Ed to get the hooks today so that she could hang them this evening.

38

The fabric was nice quality. Fairly weighty but still soft enough to hang nicely with the lining sewn in. Molly was very pleased with how they were turning out. The first curtain was almost complete and was folded neatly across the ironing board ready for the hem to be pressed into place. Molly intended to hand sew the hems with her neat, almost invisible stitching. She was currently finishing off adding the header tape to the second curtain and was guiding the fabric deftly through her sewing machine, pulling out pins as she did so and sticking them into a little velvet domed pin cushion that she'd had for years. Just as she was about to finish the final part of the machine sewing, she heard the doorbell ring. Molly was annoyed by the timing of her visitor but she would have to get up and answer the door. She dropped the foot of the machine to temporarily secure the fabric and walked through to the hallway.

'Oh Colin. Hello.' Molly hoped her smile and intonation would conceal her disappointment.

'Hello Molly. I've got those plants for you I was telling you about.'

'How kind. Thanks Colin.'

'Would you like to come over now and choose which ones you would like? I've got quite a selection.'

Molly thought it would be churlish to refuse, even though she would rather Colin had come over later in the day, but she needed to fill some gaps in the borders and finances wouldn't stretch to buying more plants at the nursery at the moment.

'I'd love to. Give me a minute. I'll fetch my shoes.'

Molly left the front door open while she went to the back porch to get her gardening shoes. It gave Colin an opportunity for a quick scan of the hallway. He noticed the bureau under the stairs with a pile of unopened post on it and a little pot with a selection of pens.

They hadn't changed the hall carpet yet but there were a selection of pictures how hanging on the walls.

'Nice paintings, Molly,' said Colin as Molly returned with shoes in hand.

'Oh yes. They're some of Ed's.'

'I didn't know he was an artist.'

Well, why you, thought Molly. None of your business.

'He loves it. Finds it relaxing,' replied Molly as she stepped out on to the doorstep and pulled on her shoes.

'Does he sell them?' asked Colin

'No. It's all just for his own enjoyment.'

Molly pulled the front door closed with enough force to signify, she hoped, that the conversation regarding Ed's artwork was now at an end.

Colin turned round and walked down the driveway towards the back garden of number three. Molly followed.

'I've got several hydrangeas, forsythia, box, lavender ... a couple of flowering currants. Other things too. You'll see anyway. Come round the back,' said Colin as he pushed open the gate at the side of his house.

'All grown from cuttings.'

Colin led the way along the garden path to the large greenhouse which was at the end of his back garden. Molly was grateful for the warmth inside as she had been shivering slightly as they had crossed Redridge Close. She noticed how orderly and clean everything was and she felt a little ashamed that she had expected it to be otherwise.

'Here's a box,' said Colin, picking up an empty cardboard box from underneath the staging.

'Help yourself to whatever you want. As you can see, I have plenty to spare.'

'I'm impressed,' replied Molly, genuinely.

'I would certainly like a couple of hydrangeas if you don't mind. And these lavender look really lovely. May I have one of those too?'

'Course you can. Here you go. Here's the lavender,' said Colin passing Molly a plant which she tucked into one corner of the box.

'Which hydrangeas? These two alright?' Colin held up two pots containing some healthy looking examples.

'They're super. Thank you.'

'Have a look at those weigela at the end there. Do you like them? They will get quite big though.'

'They are lovely. Pink flowers? And I think I could keep them in check with a good prune, couldn't I?'

'Yes, they're tough old things. Cut them back hard after they've finished flowering. And pink flowers, yes.'

'Well I would be very grateful for one of those too,' said Molly.

'Just grab a bag from under there,' said Colin, pointing under the shelves to Molly's right hand side.

As Molly bent down to pull out an old, but serviceable, hessian bag she felt something brush against the top of her thigh. She stood upright quickly and turned round. Colin appeared completely oblivious.

'That's it. I don't think I'll have room for any more. Thanks Colin.'

Molly put the weigela into the bag, put the handles over her forearm and picked up the box.

'Let me help you, Molly. Pass me the box,' said Colin.

'No, I can manage. Thanks again,' said Molly leaving the greenhouse and walking swiftly back along the path and across the close to number eleven.

39

Woolworths had a fine selection of haberdashery on the first floor, just as Molly had explained, and Edward easily selected the required curtain hooks. Having no further errands to run or purchases to make, he retraced his steps back to the office. The town was busy but it didn't take him long to get back to the second floor of the council offices. By the time he arrived at his desk, Mayhew was there, lolling back in his chair and slurping strong tea from a chipped, shiny brown, slightly grubby, mug. There was an empty sandwich tin in front of him and crumbs strewn across the desk.

'Cup of tea?' Mayhew asked Edward.

'Don't worry. I'll get myself one in a minute,' replied Edward who knew that Mayhew's offer to make tea was only just another diversionary tactic from the work which they needed to complete before 2.30pm. But that realisation gave Edward an idea.

'Are you familiar with the workings of the Hillman Imp?'

'Odd question, but yes, I suppose so. Reasonably familiar,' replied Mayhew, taking another slurp of hot tea.

'Excellent.' Reasonably familiar is familiar enough, thought Edward.

'Well when you've finished your tea, get down to the car park and take a look at the blue Imp which is on the second row in from the back, five spaces along. It's making a funny noise apparently.' Edward fished out Jennifer's keys from his jacket pocket and placed them on top of the crumbs.

Everyone would be satisfied with this solution, thought Edward triumphantly. I can get on with finishing this work in peace, Mayhew gets out of helping with it and Jennifer has her Hillman Imp examined for strange noises - even though Edward doubted their existence.

40

The end of summer holidays arrived three weeks days after the Greenacre's car had been washed clean of a picture of cat and its bodily waste. The new school term commenced and Molly was secretly pleased that the girls would be off her hands so that she could get back into the routine she so enjoyed – taking care of the house, doing the gardening and looking after Edward.

Rebecca moved up to the Comprehensive school and instantly felt uncomfortable, out of place and on occasion, terrified. Not that she told her mother that. She just accepted it as her lot. One particular group of girls at Eastfields Comprehensive had already, in the first week of term, picked out Becky as 'different' and therefore suitable victim material. They teased Becky viciously, pulling her long blonde ponytail or grabbing her leather satchel from her and swinging it round before hurling it on to the playground. Her older sister observed some of this behaviour but in such a huge school and with the different year groups using the playground at different times, not all of the abuse was witnessed. Enough though. Enough for Lizzie to see that her younger sister was already on the receiving end of the same kind of treatment she was. While the sisters fought and argued a great deal at home, it was upsetting for Lizzie to watch Becky being picked on and initially she told herself it was just first week of term 'showing off' and a hierarchy sorting itself out. She hoped it would pass. If it didn't pass, she didn't know what to do. It would be pointless telling her mother or father as they would 'make a scene' at the school and that would exacerbate the problem. The school staff wouldn't do anything, even if she told them. They hadn't protected her, so why would they protect her younger sister? It was clear their approach was to ignore such behaviour and let those sort of issues be resolved without adult intervention.

Apart from witnessing the unpleasantness of her younger sister's situation, the new term was uneventful for Elizabeth Greenacre. Uneventful was the best she could hope for. She had a new form teacher who was no better or worse than the one before and she continued to enjoy English and Art more than the other subjects. Helen was in the same sets as her which was a plus point. Following the house move, there was the new routine of the journey to get accustomed to – some days Edward would be able to drive them on his way to work, but on others they would have to get the bus. Lizzie was nervous about getting the bus at first as she didn't know if any of the nasty girls would be using the same route, but after three days of bus usage, and no sight of them, she was fairly confident she could relax a little on that score. The worse thing about using the bus was that the weather had changed and walking up the hill to the bus stop, and then hanging around waiting for it when it was cold and windy was not a pleasant experience - especially when the cold wind was blowing the steelworks stench in a south-easterly direction.

Despite all the downsides of Eastfields Comprehensive, Lizzie still got a certain amount of satisfaction from studying and acquiring knowledge. In Biology, in the second week of the autumn term, she had been set a piece of homework about essential vitamins and minerals required by the human body. She had researched the subject thoroughly, using books in the school library, and had set out her findings neatly and comprehensively in her exercise book, even adding detailed drawings of which foodstuffs provided which dietary elements. In Maths, her teacher had spent several lessons concentrating on trigonometry and Lizzie surprised herself by enjoying the problem solving tasks they were given – working out angles and areas from basic information and then drawing diagrams to show how they had reached their answers.

Becky was also an able student, but much of the first week for the first years was spent on administration and 'settling in' to senior school. During lesson time she felt safe, but dreaded the bell announcing a break period. This would mean trying to evade her aggressors - in the corridors or in the playground. It would also entail having to endure a school lunch. Her mother had told her she had to try the lunches first, before she would consider giving her a packed lunch. Becky found the smell of the school canteen repugnant, especially on the days kidneys and scrambled eggs or luncheon meat fritters were served.

Alongside the challenge of finding something vaguely edible, there was also the trauma of which seat to choose. She soon worked out that she should avoid empty tables, or tables where existing diners had nearly finished their meals. There was the opportunity for the nasty girls to sit next to her if she made that mistake. The better option was to tag on to a table which was almost full, and hopefully where there weren't too many scary and loud boys. Becky's early days at her new school were primarily a self-preservation exercise.

41

Autumn continued in much the same vein. The Greenacre sisters spent a lot of time trying to avoid confrontation at school, Molly carried on with domestic duties and trying to avoid the resident at number three and Edward kept his nose to the grindstone, conversing with Mr Jameson's secretary only when it was absolutely necessary. There was only one bright spot in those first few weeks of autumn – Molly's birthday. Edward took them all out to a nice restaurant for a meal and told the girls they could choose whatever they wanted from the menu. He presented Molly with a beautiful opal and diamond ring and she was genuinely moved by such a generous gesture.

'Did you choose this yourself?' she asked.

'Of course I did, silly,' said Edward. 'Do you like it?'

'I love it. It's beautiful. Thank you so much Ed.'

Molly slipped the ring on to her finger and held out her hand in front of her to admire it.

'I've got a present for you too,' said Lizzie.

'How exciting,' said Molly taking the small neatly wrapped parcel from her eldest daughter. She pulled off the paper to reveal a little tray of four different colour eyeshadows.

'Thanks Lizzie,' Molly exclaimed. 'That's a really lovely present. Very thoughtful.'

42

'Oh hello dear,' said Molly as Edward arrived home from work one day in late October. 'How's your day been?'

'A bit mixed, I think we'll call it. We saw the contractors this morning for our weekly meeting. Everything is on schedule and progressing fairly well. They're a good bunch of lads. Then this afternoon we were out surveying some of the houses we couldn't access earlier for one reason or another.'

Edward took off his jacket, hung it on the hook by the door and loosened his tie.

'Cup of tea?' asked Molly, stirring cheese into a sauce she was making.

'No thanks. I'm going to get myself a beer if that's alright.' Edward said as he opened the fridge and pushed aside a jar of marmalade to reach a bottle of pale ale which he had brewed himself.

'You wouldn't believe how some people choose to live Molly. Dear oh dear. We went to a house on North Park Avenue for our last call of the day. A man in his thirties I imagine, with a great big Alsatian dog. Beautiful animal. Bark far worse than his bite but the house absolutely stank. Piles of dog poo in the hall. I'm not kidding. It was unbelievable.'

The bottle of beer hissed as its cap was eased off with a bottle opener.

'Oh that's horrible,' replied Molly, the look of disgust evident on her face. She really didn't want a discussion about dog poo when she was in the middle of preparing food.

'Most of the tenants have been perfectly nice,' Edward continued, pouring the cold beer carefully into a glass. 'You know, happy to show us around, listen to what the plans are, offer to make us a drink and so on. A fair proportion of them have even spent their own money on improvements, which in a council house, is admirable, I'd say'.

Edward took a sip of his delicious beer.

'There's just the odd few who behave in ways you can't understand. Scruffy devils or aggressive even, when all we are trying to do is improve their standard of living. I have to say though that Alsatian Man wasn't confrontational. He just seemed happy to live with the stench of shit. Bit odd to say the least.'

He took another mouthful of the clear amber liquid.

Becky, whose bedroom door was ajar, had been listening to the conversation taking place between her parents. For some time she had been trying to persuade her parents to get a puppy. Her friend Sharon from Brownies where they used to live had a dog; a black Labrador called Sasha. Sasha was a permanently happy animal with an exquisitely shiny coat and large velvet ears which flapped around when Sharon and Becky had taken her out for walks across the park on Winchester Road. The girls would tie her up on the railings whilst they played on the swings and the roundabout and Sasha would sit patiently waiting for them, only standing up to wag her tail and stare expectantly at anyone passing close by in case they felt inclined to stroke her head and say hello. Becky was certain that Sasha had never done a poo in the hallway of Sharon's parents' house, not even when she was a puppy. She was a good dog and Becky felt a sudden stab of sadness in her chest when she remembered those fun-filled sunny afternoons in the park with Sharon and Sasha and realised that she would probably never see either of them again.

'Anyway, how about you? How's your day been?' enquired Edward of Molly.

'Rebecca's been off school, so I've been at home all day.'

'Oh. What's up?'

'She got herself ready for school this morning. Uniform on, satchel packed, PE kit ready and off she went with Lizzie as normal. Then five minutes later she's back in the house saying she feels ill. Tummy ache, feeling sick, and a headache apparently. I sent her off to bed and she's been there all day. I don't know Ed. I don't think there's anything at all wrong with her. She hasn't actually been sick and I've taken her temperature. It's completely normal. If she seems alright in the morning, I shall pack her off to school no matter how much complaining she does.'

Becky turned over in bed onto her right hand side, clasped her hand over her left ear and wept into the cold pillow.

The following day, Rebecca Greenacre knew that there was no point in complaining of any ailment. Her mother didn't question her regarding her state of health, just got her up at the usual time, handed her some clean school clothes and asked her to hurry up and get ready. Lizzie and Becky went off to Eastfields on the bus as normal and endured another school day; boring for the most part with elements of unpleasantness thrown in between lessons. At the end of the day the bell sounded. It was 3.40pm again, thank goodness. The sisters had got into a routine of meeting up at the back of the main block so that they could walk over to the bus together and this had been their usual rendezvous since Becky joined her sister at Eastfield Comprehensive a few weeks earlier. They usually arrived at their meeting point within a few minutes of each other depending on the proximity of their respective classrooms for last lesson. Today Becky was there first. As Lizzie approached she saw the regular group of vindictive girls taunting Becky and the ringleader pulling Becky's hair again. She was still several metres away so couldn't hear what they were saying, but sensed it was not pleasant, and she could see her sister trying to physically squirm her way out of the confrontation. Without thinking, Lizzie dropped her satchel, ran several paces at speed towards her sister's attacker, grabbed her by the shoulders, and spun her round.

'LEAVE. MY. SISTER. ALONE.'

Each word spoken loudly and forcibly, and each one synchronised beautifully with a strong rhythmic shake of the girl's nasty shoulders. Lizzie then pushed the girl as hard as she could to the side of the path where she fell back on to a collection of metal school dustbins, one of them tipping over and clanking noisily against the concrete. There was no retaliation from the gang. They were shocked to see their aggression being challenged, especially from such a previously weak source. Lizzie was even more surprised. The anger in her had risen without warning, as had the courage. Now her heart was beating fast and she was shaking so hard she struggled to pick up her satchel. As the other gang members helped their leader to her feet and righted the metal dustbin, Lizzie grabbed her sister by the arm and steered her hurriedly towards the school gates where the school buses were lined up. The sisters boarded the bus quickly and within a few minutes it set off down the hill, passing the rows of shabby houses and shops and the pavements with their copious amounts of litter, as usual. Becky wanted to ask Lizzie if she had seen the gang trying to trip her up before they started pulling her hair; she didn't know how much her elder sister had actually witnessed before launching the rather splendid retaliation, but she looked at Lizzie's frightened face and in turn that made her feel afraid too. She thought it best not to talk about it. Neither of them felt in any way victorious. Lizzie's reprisal had shocked Becky and, indeed, her attackers, but the person most surprised by the counterattack was Lizzie herself. If her mother ever found out what had just happened, Elizabeth Greenacre would be in so much trouble.

43

Colin stood in his front room in darkness. Everyone else who was at home now had their lights on. Earlier, just before it got dark, Colin had seen the Greenacre sisters walking along the close towards home after presumably getting off the bus up on the main road. Opposite he could see Martin and Glenda in their front room chatting and drinking tea. Every so often Glenda would get up and disappear. Colin imagined she was going into the kitchen to check on her pork chops. He had bumped into Glenda on her way back from the shops earlier. She wasn't inclined to stop and chat for long in the cold November air, but Colin did manage to ascertain that two pork chops had been purchased at the butchers and would be cooked for tonight's supper, along with potatoes and cabbage. Next door to them, Mrs Barrett had just shuffled over to the corner of her room and put on her standard lamp. The next house along had net curtains and the one after that was owned by Bill and Doreen Mitchell. They too had their front room lights on but annoyingly had already closed the curtains. Bill was a funny old sod in Colin's opinion. Not very sociable and neither was Doreen, although she was better and more chatty when she was on her own. Colin checked his wall clock through the gloom of the sitting room. It was hanging above the bookcase and was making a reassuring regular loud tick. Colin squinted and could see that sometime within the next ten minutes Edward Greenacre would drive past, park his car at the bottom of his driveway, get out, open the garage door, get back in the car and manoeuvre it into its allotted parking spot. All safe and secure overnight. Molly hadn't yet put her sitting room lights on, but there was light filtering through from the kitchen. She'd be in there preparing supper for her family, Colin surmised. One of the two front bedroom lights was on. That would be the older one's room. Colin had seen her in there. Her bedroom door was opposite the window and it was closed. The other two windows at the front of the house on the first floor were Edward and Molly's bedroom. Colin had seen the lights go on around ten thirty each night and witnessed Edward pulling the curtains shut. They were different curtains now. Thicker and the light was less able to penetrate. Colin was about to check the lighting and curtain status of the remaining houses which did not possess net curtains when Edward's car arrived in the close. Just as predicated, Edward put the car away into the garage before entering through the front door. Several minutes went by before he saw Edward appear in the sitting room, put on two table lights and draw the curtains. The next three nights followed pretty much the same pattern, with the exception of being able to discover what Glenda was preparing in her kitchen. November was a cruel month for those wanting to converse with their neighbours. No-one was outside cutting their grass or washing their cars. It was all scurrying inside as fast as they could, getting out of the cold and into their warm, snug houses. Next month might be better, there would be Christmas trees and bright twinkly lights around the windows and people would be all festive and jolly.

44

'Helen's Mum has asked if we want to go round on Wednesday and watch the wedding on their television.'

Lizzie had come home from school with this information after several days which had been completely clear of bullying. The clanking dustbin incident had granted a temporary reprieve it seemed.

'Oh, that's very kind of her,' replied Molly. 'Let's do that. Daddy won't come. He's not interested in that sort of thing, but me, you and Becky can go. Yes, tell Mrs Burrows we would love to do that.'

Molly was pleased that she would be spending time in the company of another seemingly like-minded woman. She had only met Helen's mother twice before, the first occasion being when they had passed each other in the school corridor during parents evening. They had introduced themselves, briefly exchanged pleasantries and instantly warmed to each other. A few weeks later, Sylvia Burrows had collected Helen from 78 Wordsworth Close after her daughter had come round after school, supposedly to do some biology homework with Lizzie, although the delights of Marc Bolan and either of the Davids (Bowie or Cassidy) may have prevented the girls' full concentration on cell structure and division. Molly didn't invite Helen's mother in as she was ashamed to admit this was their home and she was well aware that the Burrows family lived at the opposite end of the town where the houses were detached and well-kept. Sylvia Burrows had been friendly, confident and polite. She was unfazed and there was no trace of any kind of judgemental attitude towards the Greenacre's current place of abode. Molly could sense that they would get on well.

'Oh hello Ed,' said Molly as her husband walked into the kitchen. Lizzie and I were just talking about Wednesday. The wedding. Helen's Mum has invited us over to watch it there. I take it you won't be interested.'

'Definitely not! Damn waste of public time and money. Look at the state this country is in at the moment what with the oil crisis, strikes and stock market crashing. No thanks.'

Molly had been expecting this response and, without responding to her husband, turned her attention back to her eldest daughter.

'Ask Mrs Burrows what time we should arrive and also whether she wants me to bring anything. I could make a sponge cake and take that perhaps.'

'I'll ask Helen tomorrow.'

45

There was widespread excitement building throughout the whole country for the wedding of Princess Anne to Captain Mark Phillips and the day had been declared a national holiday. This was going to be the biggest royal event since the coronation of the queen twenty years earlier.

On the morning of Wednesday 14th November, Edward dropped off Molly and the girls at Sylvia Burrows house. Helen was waiting for their arrival and stood watching from the windows of the sitting room at the front.

'They're here,' she called through to her mother when she saw Edward pull into the driveway.

'Let them in then would you please Helen?' called Sylvia from the kitchen.

Molly and the girls entered the house and were shown through to the large and comfortable sitting room by Helen. Sylvia soon joined them.

'Let me take that from you, Molly' she said.

Molly handed over a sponge cake which she had made the previous day and filled with strawberry jam just before they set off this morning.

'Helen. Can you take Mrs Greenacre's coat? Take it upstairs and put it on the spare bed. Lizzie and Becky - you can put yours there too.'

The three girls ran upstairs, chatting happily, leaving Molly and Sylvia in the sitting room.

'So today not your husband's cup of tea?' asked Sylvia.

'Not exactly!'

'Well, I imagine it was met with the same response I got from Helen's Dad. Unenthusiastic I think you would call it at best. We're going to enjoy it though. Let the men carry on doing whatever they want to do – mine's clattering spanners and wrenches against a dirty old motorcycle in the garage today!'

Sylvia turned round and switched on the television. She looked at her watch.

'Twenty minutes yet before the coverage starts. Come through to the kitchen and we'll make a pot of tea.'

Molly liked Sylvia's easy attitude and could see why Helen was such a good friend to Lizzie.

'Sylvia opened the cake tin for a quick peek inside.

'It looks delicious! Thank you.'

Sylvia reached down into one of the kitchen cupboards and brought out five plates.

'Now what can I get you? Tea or coffee?'

'I would love some tea please,' replied Molly looking round at the slightly dated but bright and clean kitchen.

'How lovely that you've got these double doors opening up on to the garden,' she commented.

'Yes, it's a nice aspect. We're very lucky. Won't be opening the doors today though! Bit chilly for that!' Sylvia put the kettle on the gas hob and reached for two cups from the shelf on the wall.

'I wonder if Princess Anne will be wearing a winter coat over her wedding dress?' Molly laughed.

'Well even that would be better than jodphurs! Anyway, I don't suppose she'll be outside for long, will she?' replied Sylvia. 'She'll probably roll up in one of those ornate carriage things and go straight in to the Abbey. But then again, can you imagine how cold Westminster Abbey is going to be at this time of year?'

'What time of year did you get married?' Molly asked Sylvia.

'Oh, it was July. A lovely warm and sunny day. My captain was sweating buckets I seem to recall. To be honest, that was probably nerves knowing that he was about to be stuck with me for the rest of his life.'

Sylvia laughed and handed Molly the plates, some cake forks and five linen napkins.

'We were June. It was cold though. I can remember shivering through the whole service. That was probably nerves too.'

Sylvia carefully took Molly's sponge cake out of the tin and placed it on a glass cake stand.

'Look at that. It's lovely Molly. Really lovely. A beautiful wedding cake. Come on, we'll take these through to the sitting room and come back for the tea.

Molly felt comfortable already in Sylvia's home and in her company. She usually found it easy to befriend other women and at Winchester Road she had a regular group of friends; other mothers at the schools, Women's Institute members, neighbours, church members and colleagues at work. Until this moment, she hadn't realised quite how much she had missed them. She had been so caught up in two house moves and getting her family settled in this new location that her own needs, in terms of social interaction, had been put on hold. She had a good relationship with her husband and could talk to him about anything. Well almost anything. Despite that, female companionship was very important to her. Molly hadn't warmed to any of the other women she had encountered so far since arriving in Greythorpe. She was certain this was no fault of hers, or theirs even, it was just that they were on different wavelengths, living different lives with different priorities. Briefly an image of 78 Wordsworth Close came into her head. Mrs Kirby, six doors down, with her errant sons. The woman next door but one – Molly never had learned her name but she and Ed secretly called her Mrs Grime – she seemed to spend an inordinate amount of time yelling at her young children. And opposite, the mother of a child who was in the same class as Becky and appeared unable to smile, even though Molly had said good morning to her on several occasions when they followed the same route to school. At Redridge Close the neighbours were friendly enough but Molly just hadn't found any common ground with them. None of her female neighbours seemed particularly interested in her and Molly certainly wasn't one for forcing herself on to others. In any case, Molly thought, they were probably all busy people, with families and jobs and houses to take care of. Friendships she had made in the past had been forged from a natural and uncomplicated connection. Like this one, now. She could tell that Sylvia was the kind of person with whom she would enjoy spending time.

While Sylvia and Molly were in the front room rearranging the furniture in order that everyone would get a good view of the television, the kettle began to whistle loudly and spit blobs of boiling water over the hob. Sylvia called up the stairs as they walked back along the elegant hallway to the kitchen. 'Girls – come downstairs in about ten minutes, alright?'

In the kitchen Molly saw a tea tray on the worktop which Sylvia had left out ready. Molly put the cups on to it while Sylvia poured water into the teapot.

'Can you find me three glasses for squash from the dresser please?' asked Sylvia. 'Oh, and that jug too please.'

Molly turned to the welsh dresser behind her and lifted the glasses carefully off the shelf.

'Bung them on the tray Molly. Thanks.' She held up two bottles of squash. 'Blackcurrant or orange?'

'Blackcurrant,' said Molly. 'It's a more regal colour.'

Sylvia made up a jug of purple squash and handed it to Molly.

'Can you take this for me and I'll bring the tray?'

Molly followed Sylvia back along the hallway and they sat down ready to watch the proceedings. The three girls joined them and were each handed a glass of regal squash and a slice of cake.

'Here we go, then' said Sylvia, leaning across to turn the volume dial on the television up a little as the Scottish Coach emerged from Buckingham Palace carrying the Queen, the Queen Mother, the Prince of Wales and Prince Andrew.

'Look at those horses Mummy,' said Becky.

'Beautiful, aren't they?' replied Molly.

'Ooooo – here comes Princess Anne,' said Sylvia. In the glass coach. Very fancy.'

It's not glass,' said Helen. 'It looks black to me. And look at all those people standing around on the street.'

'You do have to wonder why they're there, don't you?' laughed Molly. 'We've got a much better view here.'

'We certainly have,' replied Sylvia. 'We're in the warm and we've got cake too,' she continued, putting a large forkful of the delicious sponge into her mouth.

'Oh my goodness Molly,' said Sylvia with a mouthful. 'That is good cake.'

'How far do they have to go in that so called glass coach? Are they off to some castle somewhere?' asked Lizzie.

'Oh it's not far Lizzie. Less than a mile. They're going to Westminster Abbey,' replied her mother.

'What?' exclaimed Lizzie. 'Less than a mile and they've gone to all that trouble getting the glass coach out, hooking up the horses, getting the other coach out – what's it called again – oh yes, the Scottish coach – more horses – just to go a mile? Less than a mile?'

Sylvia and Molly both laughed and couldn't argue a case for going to 'all that trouble' other than the fact it was tradition.

'That's the spectacle people want to see Lizzie. They want a princess in a royal coach with horses and soldiers all dressed up in their colourful tunics and all the regalia, pomp and ceremony.'

In between stuffing mouthfuls of victoria sponge into their mouths, the three girls watched the proceedings with genuine interest, although, on Lizzie and Becky's part, this was sparked by the fact the television was a colour one and they had only seen those in shop windows before.

'Mr and Mrs Peter Phillips at the great west door,' repeated Sylvia, who had been paying attention to the commentator.

'Look at her posh hat with feathers all blowing around in the breeze. I wonder what she's thinking right now.'

'She's thinking, my boy has done alright for himself, I would say,' said Molly and both women laughed.

'Look at that man with his funny white socks,' said Becky.

'That's a footman,' said Molly.

'A footman? Foot. Man,' repeated Becky. 'Funny name for a man wearing girls' socks and shoes.'

'Is that the queen?' asked Helen.

'Yes.'

'Where's her crown?' asked Becky.

'She doesn't wear a crown every day Becky. It's just for special occasions.'

'Isn't this a special occasion?'

'Clearly not special enough,' laughed Sylvia.

'Who is the old lady with the bag?' asked Helen.

'It's the Queen Mother. Princess Anne's grandma,' replied Sylvia.

'Funny,' said Helen. 'She doesn't look much like a grandma.'

'Hang on everyone,' said Sylvia wiping up the remaining crumbs from her plate with her forefinger. 'The bride is on her way.'

The assembled audience remained silent while they watched Princess Anne arrive and alight from the non-glass glass coach.

'Silk. Pure white. Embroidered. Voluminous sleeves. Big veil.' Sylvia gave a precis of the finer sartorial points.

'Very nice,' said Molly. 'It is quite simple, but very elegant, wouldn't you say?'

'She looks lovely,' agreed Sylvia.

'Funny hat,' said Lizzie who had just caught a glimpse of the bridesmaid.

'Funny skirt,' laughed Helen, looking at the page boy.

'Prince Andrew?' said Sylvia, correcting the commentator. 'Prince Andrew? He's got that wrong. It's Prince Edward – the littlest one.'

'Anne's smiling, look,' said Molly. 'She doesn't look at all nervous, does she?'

'She looks incredibly calm actually. You're right Molly. Maybe this is a walk in the park after competing in those horse riding thingies.'

'Prince Philip's going a bit thin on top. Look at the top of his bonce,' continued Sylvia.

'Oh yes,' said Molly. 'I see what you mean. We don't often see him from this angle, do we?'

'Here we go now. Here's the groom. Captain Phillips. He still has a good head of hair at least.'

'Yes. And so smart in his military uniform. Very dapper,' said Molly.

Everyone fell silent again as they listened to the happy couple say their vows. For better for worse. For richer for poorer. In sickness and in health. Molly repeated them herself – in her head. Several times over.

'That man with the funny hat has got a wobbly voice,' remarked Becky.

'It's the Archbishop of Canterbury and his hat is called a mitre,' Molly informed Becky quietly.

'Let no man put asunder,' said Sylvia in a mocking Archbishop of Canterbury wobbly voice.

Molly stifled a laugh as she felt it would be a bit disrespectful to giggle out loud, not to mention setting a bad example to the girls.

'That's it,' said Sylvia to the new Mrs Phillips on the television. 'You've gone and done it now girl.'

While the register was being signed, Sylvia got up to make another pot of tea.

'Any more squash girls?'

'No thanks,' said Helen. 'Could we have some more cake though please?'

'Of course you can,' replied Molly. 'Pass your plates and I'll cut you another slice.'

Plates and tea cups were recharged and everyone sat back to watch the newly married couple take a long walk to the West Door and get in the carriage to take them back to Buckingham Palace.

Molly and Sylvia appreciated the grand organ music and the way in which the Princess' veil was caught by the breeze as she approached the doorway and it flowed out behind her. They saw her and her new husband get into the coach and heard the bells ringing out from the Abbey.

Neither Molly nor Sylvia realised it, but they were both sitting there smiling as they watched the coach pull away and head off through the crowded streets, lined with people cheering and waving flags. The horses pulled the coach expertly around the Victoria Memorial and the cheers from the crowds seemed to get louder. The coverage showed the royal couple get out of the coach and enter the palace.

'Why is he carrying a sword, Mummy?' asked Becky.

'He's a soldier. A captain in the British Army,' replied Molly.

'He won't need a sword today though, will he?'

'Not unless he wants to chop off the queen's head,' said Helen.

'Helen!' scolded Sylvia, although she was smiling as she briefly imagined Captain Mark Phillips emerging on to the balcony balancing the queen's head on the end of his shiny sword and blue blood dripping down his arm.

'I wonder if he has actually stabbed anyone with it though?' mused Helen.

'Of course he hasn't,' replied Sylvia. 'It's just for show. Part of his official uniform.'

'Well if I ever get married, I won't let my husband carry a sword unless he has actually used it. Several times,' said Helen.

'I do hope you're not planning on marrying a serial killer, Helen. It's not exactly how your father and I envisaged your life turning out.'

46

'Should we reinstate Saturday Night Nosh Night?' Edward asked Molly one morning, a few days later.

'I mean we've got more space now to all sit round the table properly and I've set up the record player.'

'Yes, why not? We'll do it this weekend, shall we?' replied Molly.

Saturday Night Nosh Night had been a regular feature of the Greenacre household at 186 Winchester Road. Molly would cook something extra special, often trying new recipes which might include an exotic ingredient like garlic or avocado pear, and Edward would buy a bottle of nice wine. The dining table would be set with the 'special' tablecloth, the best crockery and cutlery and the 'posh' table mats. There would be candles in the centre of the table, linen napkins in silver napkin rings and fresh flowers in a little glass vase. Four crystal wine glasses would be placed on coasters which Edward neatly lined up perfectly with the table mats. Lizzie and Becky were often given a small glass of wine to try when Edward and Molly were drinking it. It was how Edward's parents had introduced him to fine wine and it was his pleasure to do the same with the next generation.

When Saturday evening arrived and the table had been laid, the Greenacre Family assembled themselves in the sitting room.

'The dinner is almost ready,' said Molly. 'Ed dear, do you want to put some music on?'

Edward walked across to the record player, lifted the lid and gently picked up the arm to blow dust, real or imagined, from the stylus.

'What shall we listen to Molly? Any requests?' Edward asked.

'I don't mind dear. You choose.'

Edward selected an LP entitled 'Caribbean Carnival' from the cupboard below the player.

'Magic rhythms of calypso, blue beat and steel band,' Edward read aloud from the album cover. 'Russ Henderson and his Caribbean Boys. Come on then Russ and your boys. Let's hear you. We haven't played you in a while.'

On a similar theme, Edward also chose 'South Sea Island Magic' and by way of complete contrast 'March', a collection of military band music and 'The World of Mantovani'. Edward's eclectic musical appreciation was evident. He stacked the records and placed them on to the spindle, then set the turntable spinning at the required thirty three revolutions per minute. The first long player dropped down on to the turntable, the arm moved across and Ray Blair, one of Russ' boys, commenced his rendition of 'Walking the Dog'.

'Here we go then,' said Molly, placing the first course of melon and orange on to the table. A decorative piece of orange had been secured with a cocktail stick into the melon and had a cocktail cherry atop. The family gathered at the table to enjoy the first Nosh Night for several months. Edward poured the wine, walking round the table to fill everyone's glass, with a tea towel over his arm pretending that he was a waiter in a restaurant.

'Can I tempt you to some of our finest Claret, madam?'

The melon, orange and ginger starter smelled fresh and sweet and the family began their meal.

'This is delicious Molly,' said Edward.

'And while we're all here together, now might be a good time to tell you girls about something that's happening next week.'

Lizzie and Becky looked at their father as it was obviously going to be good news.

'I've arranged to have a new television delivered. A colour one.'

'A colour one? Really?' said Lizzie

'Yes, really. It's coming on Tuesday afternoon.'

Up until now the only colour televisions Lizzie and Becky had seen had been in Helen's house or the electrical shops in the town. The Greenacres, and other families, would halt their progress along the high street to briefly hover round the shop windows and admire this wonderful new technology. Molly secretly thought the acquisition of a colour television was an extravagance and a luxury they could do without, but Edward had made the decision and he was looking forward to watching Dickie Davies presenting 'World of Sport' on Saturday afternoons. Dickie's magnificent head of hair, his brown suit, and huge collar and tie would be resplendent in full colour.

'Will it be here when we get home from school?' asked Becky.

'Should be,' replied Edward.

'Oh good. I'll be able to watch 'Blue Peter' not in black and white.'

The family finished their starter and Molly cleared away the empty dishes. While she was busy in the kitchen dishing up the main course, Edward and the girls were listening to track four of 'Caribbean Carnival', a delightfully cheery number; the lyrics conveying a story about a man who went out drinking then got home and beat his wife. Anyway, she takes her revenge by hitting him on the head with a rolling pin, a pot and a frying pan and now, here he is, lying stone cold dead in the market place. It's alright though as he had it coming to him, and she hadn't killed anyone else apart from him. The finer nuances of the song may have been lost on Lizzie and Becky but they loved joining in with the verse about the frying pan.

47

It was after one such Nosh Night in early December that the Greenacres decided to take a walk before clearing the table and washing up. As usual they had enjoyed wonderful food and amusing music.

'It's only half past eight,' said Edward.

'Shall we have a little walk before tidying up? I think I could do with some fresh air. I know it's cold and icy but we'll be alright if we tog up with coats and scarves.'

'Do we have to go out, Daddy?' asked Becky.

'Yes, come on. We won't be long. Just round the block to walk our dinner down.'

'It doesn't need walking down. It's gone down.'

Molly handed Becky her coat. 'Put this on please. Your scarf and gloves are here too look. Daddy's right. We could all do with some fresh air.'

The family left the house by the front door, Edward locking it securely behind them.

The sky was completely clear and the air was still but felt icy cold against their faces. The streetlights illuminated the front gardens of their neighbours, where the plants and grass were sparkling with frost. Molly pulled her coat tighter around her. As they passed Number Three, Molly could see Colin watching television in his front room, curtains wide open and his chair carefully positioned so that he could watch the screen and see all that was happening in the close at the same time. She looked away and the carried on to the end of the close.

'Which way shall we go?' she asked as they reached the main road.

'I think if we go left down the hill, we can then cut back along Aldiss Avenue and back up past the church. It's probably going to take us around thirty minutes to do that route. Just about right.'

The houses along the hill leading away from Redridge Close were silent and obviously closed up for the evening. Their curtains were drawn tight against the winter night, lit up from behind by lamps and television sets. When the Greenacres reached the junction with Aldiss Avenue, they turned left.

'See that house over there,' said Lizzie, pointing. 'I think that's the one where that teacher who got the sack lives.'

Molly wasn't sure that the rumours about a teacher being sacked were true but nevertheless turned around to take a look at the house. As she did so she lost her footing on the icy kerb and fell to the ground.

'Ed. My arm,' she cried.

Edward immediately rushed to his wife's aid. He was shocked and extremely concerned. He took hold of her uninjured arm and lifted her back to her feet.

'My arm. I felt it go. I need to sit down Ed. I feel really sick.'

'Sit on this wall, here,' said Edward, guiding his wife across the pavement. His voice was calm and kind.

Molly was crying and held her left forearm with her other hand. She sat down on the garden wall and rocked back and forth. 'It's so painful,' she sobbed, her voice cracking with pain. 'I felt it go. I think it's broken Ed.'

Lizzie and Becky, who were both feeling scared, stood back a little from where their mother was sitting. They had never seen her cry before.

'Don't worry Molly,' said Edward quickly but gently.

'We'll get this sorted out. I'm going to run back up the hill and fetch the car. We'll get you into the hospital. Girls, stay with your mother. I'll be as quick as I can.'

Edward, who was not one for moving quickly under normal circumstances, ran as fast as he could back up to Redridge Close and unlocked the garage. As he ran, he tried to remember how much petrol there was in the car. This was the age of the oil crisis and rationing had been considered, but Edward always tried to keep his tank at least half full. He checked the gauge as he backed out. They would be alright. Just under half a tank. Within a matter of minutes he had returned to his family and helped Molly into the front seat of the car.

There was not much traffic on the road and Edward was able to drive quickly but safely to the hospital.

48

'May I take the patient's name?' asked the young woman behind the reception desk in the Emergency area.

'Molly Greenacre. Mrs,' said Edward.

'Date of Birth?'

'Seventeenth of September 1931'

'And the reason for your visit here this evening Sir?'

'An injury to her left arm, possibly broken. She fell on the icy pavement and is a considerable amount of pain now.'

'Right. And you are Mr Greenacre, I take it?'

'Correct.'

'Well if you can take a seat over there in the waiting area with your wife please, I will get someone to attend to her as soon as I can.'

'Thank you.'

Edward rejoined Molly and his daughters and checked his watch. It read quarter past nine. He wondered how long they would be kept waiting. He hated seeing Molly in pain.

'They're going to get someone to come out and see you,' he reassured his wife. 'I don't think it will be too long. Do you think we should try and get your coat off?'

Molly got slowly to her feet and Edward undid the buttons for her. She had stopped crying now but her face was pale and tear stained. She wriggled her uninjured arm free from the sleeve and Edward very carefully pulled on the other sleeve so that Molly could slip out of the coat. She winced as Edward took up the weight of the garment and lifted it away from her.

'Sorry Molly. It's off now. Here, sit down again.'

Edward looked at Molly's swollen forearm and then back at his watch again.

After just a few minutes came the call they had been waiting for.

'Molly Greenacre please.'

Edward got to his feet and signalled to the nurse who had called out Molly's name.

'If you'd like to come with me please,' the nurse said to Molly, smiling as she approached.

'Sir, I shall have to ask you to wait here please. We're going to take a look at this arm. I will be back later to let you know what's going on.'

'Thank you,' said Edward, placing his hand gently on Molly's back as she got to her feet and was led away by the nurse.

Edward sat back down with Lizzie and Becky. They were all tired and drained by the events of the evening and sat quietly, none of them having the energy or wishing to engage in conversation with each other. From the hilarity of the frying pan song to the terrifying atmosphere of a hospital in less than an hour.

49

Over the space of just a few hours Mrs Lillian Greenacre noticed her young son becoming weak and listless, losing his appetite and then becoming feverish. When a large lump appeared on the neck of her tiny distressed child she immediately knew what that meant and she was terrified. Several children in the streets around the area where they lived had caught the infection and quite a few of them had not survived. When the tuberculosis diagnosis was confirmed, and treatment for Edward had been decided, his mother tried to explain it to him in words that could be understood by a four year old.

'There are some lovely doctors and nurses who are going to help you to get better Eddie. They work in a hospital near the seaside so Daddy and I are going to take you there. You will stay there for a few weeks or months until you are well again. It will all be alright, you'll see.'

Her left arm was wrapped tightly around her adored son who was sitting on her lap with his little head leaning against her chest. She was gently stroking his dark curly hair with her right hand and she could feel the heat from his painful feverish forehead.

Her voice was trembling. 'It will all be alright,' she repeated as large tears dropped off her face on to the back of her hand.

The following day Edward was taken seventy miles from South London to the hospital on the Kent coast which specialised in the treatment of the condition in children. Richard and Lillian Greenacre carried their beloved sick child into the hospital and up to the reception area. The nurse recorded some brief details and took them through to a ward where Edward was allocated a bed. The other seven beds in the ward were already occupied. Richard looked round at the other patients in their metal hospital beds and noticed how Edward's new roommates all looked pitifully small and vulnerable. Some of them were encased in full body plaster casts, able only to move their lower arms and legs. The ward was dark, the walls were painted in shiny green paint and the room smelled strongly of disinfectant. Richard could hear a nurse speaking softly to a terrified child who was sobbing in the bed nearest the large window. The child was probably no older than his own son and he instantly felt sick with fear. In the ward next door, Richard could hear other children chatting with each other, clearly not currently upset like the young boy in the corner. He took solace in that. There was also the sound of a metal bed being moved across the wooden floor. Lillian tried hard not to look around as she was already deeply distressed and consumed with concern for her own child. Leaving him behind as she and Richard drove back to London later on today was going to be the most difficult thing she had ever had to do and she was dreading it.

The accepted thinking in the treatment of this type of tuberculosis was that the patient should be kept as still as possible, hence the plaster casts. The medical staff spoke to Edward's parents with professionalism and care, explaining in detail what would happen to their son. Richard and Lillian clung to the positive elements of the information being imparted to them as their emotions swung from desperation to sanguine and back again, and then said a petrifying goodbye to their first born.

Within a few hours Edward was restrained in a plaster cast like several of the other children on the ward. At age four he was unable to grasp the severity of his condition; all he did know was that he was frightened and in pain and he longed for the tender embrace of his mother. The cast covered his entire torso and a metal bar inserted into the back of it prevented him from moving his head. There were further restraints which stopped much movement of his arms and hands, although the nurse told him that she would temporarily release these when it was time to eat. He didn't want to eat. He wanted to cry.

For many weeks Edward was restrained in the cast. He became accustomed to the routines of the ward and the regular painful draining of the lump on his neck. His parents arrived every weekend and for three short hours he would bask in the glorious attention of parental love. When they left he would sink back down into his plaster shell and sob all over again. His depression was exacerbated to excruciating levels when roommates disappeared, which happened every so often. The sombre but efficient medical staff would cover the unfortunate child with a sheet and he would be wheeled out, the bed and surrounding area scrubbed clean and made up for another patient. In later years Edward would realise that he was lucky. Over the course of the late summer and autumn his tiny diseased body began to respond to the medical treatment.

'Mrs and Mrs Greenacre? Hello. We're going to get Edward out that cast tomorrow. When you arrive next weekend you'll find him on the ward on the ground floor.'

That was the news Richard and Lillian had been waiting and praying for. Stage one of their precious son's treatment was over and he was on the path to a full recovery. They were elated.

Edward's cast was painfully sawn off and his withered but now disease free body lifted into a warm iodine bath. His ribs, collar bone and spine protruded through his white skin and his leg and arm muscles were all but useless. But he was free from the tyranny of the plaster and metal restraints! Later he was taken downstairs to a new ward which overlooked a quadrangle. Rows of metal beds were lined up in the salty open air along each of the four walls. The beds were exposed to the elements save for a wood and tile canopy above them. Each bed was made up with sheets and blankets as normal but covered with a thick red rubber sheet. That was his home for a further nine weeks; sleeping outside, no matter what the weather, enjoying plentiful and wholesome food and chatting with the other children who had been equally 'lucky' to have made it to ground floor level.

Finally Richard and Lillian got to take their child home to London, all three of them ecstatic that they were reunited and Lillian was determined that from here on she would lavish as much love upon her son as was humanly possible.

50

'Mr Greenacre please,' called a nurse from the desk in the reception area. Edward rose to his feet and picked up Molly's coat. 'Stay here girls. I don't think I'll be too long.' He walked across to the desk.

'Your wife is ready to go home now. You'll find her in Treatment Room Four, just round to the left there.'

Edward opened the door to Room Four and found Molly, smiling weakly and sitting on a chair, her left arm encased in plaster. He looked at it and tried hard to disguise his rising panic as he helped her upright and wrapped her coat around her shoulders.

'I don't know Molly. What a thing to do. Come on, let's get you home.'

'Thank you so much for all you've done for my wife,' he said to the nurse who opened the door for them. 'I'm very grateful to you. Goodnight.'

51

Edward was going to take a few days off work over the Christmas and New Year period and Molly was very pleased about that. She was finding everything difficult with the plaster cast on her arm. Cooking, cleaning, shopping, ironing, even getting bathed and dressed was so hard. It was making her irritable and she was annoyed that the Christmas she had planned – their first at Redridge Close - would now have to be adapted to suit her limited capabilities. Edward was willing, and a kind and thoughtful husband, but was unpractised in the art of home-making. His domestic skills had never been honed due to Molly's usual efficiency in that department. He would do whatever he could to help though and they would still have a good Christmas, he was sure of that. On Christmas Eve he went out with a shopping list Molly had given him and came back with almost everything correct, apart from the flour.

'Shall I go back and get another bag?' he asked Molly.

'No. Don't worry. I can make do with this. It's fine.'

'I got the girls their presents, but I've left them in the car for now,' Edward said quietly, as even though his daughters were both upstairs, he wasn't sure if their doors were open or closed.

'I'll have to ask you to wrap them for me.'

'Let's wait until they've gone to bed and then I'll bring them in and wrap them,' said Edward.

'Could you help me re-decorate the tree too?' asked Molly. 'Becky has made a right mess of it. Then there was an argument with Lizzie when she tried to help and that's the result.' Molly waved her plastered arm in the direction of the corner of the room where the bedraggled Christmas tree stood, and Edward admitted that it could do with a bit of a tidy-up.

'Tell you what, my sweet. We'll get the vegetables on for dinner and while they're doing I'll pour us both a nice Christmas Eve sherry and we'll get that tree looking magnificent. How does that sound?'

'Thanks Ed,' Molly smiled at her husband and walked through to the kitchen to see to the vegetables. She had managed to prepare a casserole for them earlier in the day with Ed's help chopping up the meat and lifting the heavy dish into the oven.

'Potatoes first,' said Molly. If you can lift that saucepan on to the gas ring for me please. Then we'll come back and do the rest.'

'They'll need salt, won't they?' asked Edward, opening several wall cupboards looking for the tub of cooking salt.

'Cupboard next to the sink,' said Molly, feeling amused that Edward still didn't know where the salt was kept.

'I called my mother this afternoon,' said Edward as he poured a small amount of salt into the pan.

'She's offering to come up and help out for a few days when I go back to work after Christmas.' He had his back to Molly as he was peering into the saucepan wondering if he had added enough salt. He decided he hadn't and added some more.

'Well, that's kind of her Ed, but I honestly think I'll be alright. I'm getting used to managing with this beast of an arm. Besides, where would she sleep? We haven't got a spare bedroom and I don't think it's fair to ask Lizzie and Becky to share. We've just got their rooms redecorated and looking nice.'

'I did tell her that I thought you would be more than capable,' Edward lied.

He'd told his mother no such thing and now he'd have to call her back and try and find a valid reason for why her services would not be necessary. It was going to require some sensitive handling.

'Come on Molly. Let's pour this sherry and make a start on that tree.'

Molly knelt down by the box of glass baubles and handed them up to Ed, directing him on their positions. He also rearranged the tinsel. As he remarked, Becky's effort made it looked like it had been fired from a catapult from the top end of the close. He also had to straighten out the angel at the top.

'Here you go, Mrs. We can't have you lolling back like that. It's not very dignified,' said Edward, addressing the little figure which had been a part of every Greenacre Christmas since 1954.

He stood back to admire his handiwork.

'What do you think Molly? Is that better?'

'Much better. Can you get the lights on for me now please? They're in that box on the sideboard.

Within half an hour, the tree was fixed, the dinner was ready and Lizzie and Becky had joined their parents for the official switch-on.

Colin stood in the gloom of his front room and watched as Edward stood next to the Christmas tree, held aloft a glass and made a toast to, presumably, his family and the season of goodwill.

52

1974 arrived just as the calendar predicted, along with the start of the government imposed three day working week. Molly secretly hoped that the steelworks would be affected as this might mean less sulphurous smell in the air. And she also decided that every time the weather was cold enough to make the footpaths icy, she would avoid going out if she could. Her arm was healing but still encased in plaster and she did not want to run the risk of falling over again. Her progress in the house with all the usual household chores was being impeded by her thick white lump of a left forearm and it was very frustrating. Things were bad enough as they were. However, today she needed to visit the local shops to buy some sugar and a box of tea. She also wanted to go to the Post Office and get some stamps. So reluctantly, she left the safety of a carpeted house so that she could gingerly make her way along the slippery pavement to the end of Redridge Close and further up the main road towards the row of shops which the Greenacres used regularly since they had moved here. Molly had put on her new winter boots. They had a good tread on the bottom and so she hoped they would offer adequate traction with the dangerous surface of the freezing cold path. She locked the front door and started to walk carefully along the close. She was concentrating so hard on remaining vertical that she didn't notice Colin at Number Three coming out of his side door and walking across the road towards her. He was within ten feet of her before she realised he was there and she was startled to find him suddenly on the path in front of her.

'Hello Molly. You've been in the wars. What happened?'

Molly's heart sank. She really did not want to stop and have a conversation with Tedious Colin. But here he was. Standing right in front of her, blocking the pavement with five foot six worth's of tiresome anecdotes encased in a slightly grubby hand-knitted fairisle jumper and trousers which finished several inches above his ankle. Odd, thought Molly, bearing in mind his diminutive stature. She would have to be polite, but she would try and keep this encounter short. Really short.

'Yes, I'm afraid I slipped over about three weeks ago and broke my wrist.' She lifted her left arm slightly to illustrate the point.

'Oh dear. You poor thing. I bet that hurt a bit. Did they fix it up for you at St Georges?'

'St Georges, yes. Fortunately there weren't too many other casualties in the Emergency Department that evening so they got me sorted fairly swiftly.'

'Must be very inconvenient having your arm in plaster, so you let me know if there's anything I can do for you now, won't you? I do know what it's like. I broke my arm once. Fell off the top rung of the ladder while I was putting new felt on the shed roof. Not the shed I've got now. My old one. The one I sold to the Johnson's at Number Nine when I bought a bigger one. They've still got it too. In good condition as well. And my goodness, my arm did smart, I can tell you. Swelled up like a balloon too. I hit the ground as hard as you like. Felt it go, I did. I think that was in 1966. Yes, that's right. 1966. I remember now because I can recall watching the football with my arm in plaster. Ah! That was a day! We showed 'em, didn't we? 4 -2. Great game. Shame about 1970. Only made it as far as the quarter finals, but I have high hopes for this year. Course, my dear wife was still alive then. God rest her soul. 'You're daft' she said. 'Never should be up a ladder at your age.' But she looked after me while I was out of action. Don't know what would happen to me if I broke it again now. No-one to look after me now.' Colin paused. 'But if there's anything you want me to help you with, you just say. Alright? And I meant what I said about using my telephone. If your Mum needs to ring you or if you have to make a call, then that's perfectly fine by me.'

'That's very kind of you, Colin. I have actually let my mother know your number' said Molly, now beginning to shiver in the bitter cold. She was anxious not to get involved in any further discussion regarding Colin's shed, football (especially football) or his late wife and moved a step forward to signify the end of the conversation.

'You know where am. Happy to help if I can,' said Colin as he stepped down into the road and turned back towards Number Three. 'You must come and see my cacti in my greenhouse when you've got a minute,' he called back over his shoulder as an afterthought.

'Thanks Colin. I'd really like that,' Molly lied.

53

'We're due another power cut this evening Molly. Do we have any candles left?' Edward was looking at the local Evening Telegraph dated 5 February where timetables of scheduled electricity black-outs were published. 'Good old Prime Minister Heath and his state of emergency!' he said, folding the paper up and putting it down on the kitchen worktop.

'We've got two half used candles from the last time,' said Molly, checking in the kitchen drawer that they were still there together with the box of matches. 'And I managed to buy another two in that hardware shop on the high street yesterday. I must have just been lucky with the timing. When I was there earlier in the week, they had completely sold out.'

'Well, I'll fetch the paraffin lamp in from the garage as well,' said Edward. 'It won't be so bad for us. It's the old folk or those with young kiddies I feel most sorry for. And for people living alone too. That can't be much fun. At least we've got a gas oven Molly. We'll do what we did last time and sit in here. It'll be chilly in the sitting room when the heating goes off. It's perishing cold outside today. But we'll manage.'

Just like many other young families, the Greenacres were feeling a strange sense of excitement about the next lot of scheduled power cuts. It was a bizarre sort of challenge. Could they keep warm enough and would it be possible to entertain themselves for the duration of the planned amount of eerie darkness?

Later that day, when the allotted time came, Lizzie, Becky and their parents sat in the kitchen round a little folding table that Edward had set up When the lights went out Edward already had the candles and the paraffin lamp glowing and in position on the worktops. Molly struck a match and bent down to ignite the gas in the oven. As the strip of blue flame shot up into life, the Greenacres cheered.

Molly left the oven door open and the heat soon warmed up the kitchen.

'Can I be Miss Scarlett this time?' asked Becky.

'Yes, here she is,' said Molly as she passed her youngest daughter the red plastic token and placed the Cluedo board on the table.

'And who are you going to be Lizzie?'

'I'll be Mrs Peacock please.'

'Edward, here's Professor Plum for you and I'll be the yellow one.'

'It's Colonel Mustard' said Lizzie as she passed the cards to Edward.

'Shuffle these please Dad and then we can each pick one card for the envelope. And no looking Becky. Cheating is not allowed.'

'I don't cheat, do I Daddy? Tell Lizzie I'm not a cheat.'

'Shush, both of you,' said Molly. 'Let's just have a nice game.'

Edward shuffled the cards and three cards were selected for the special little envelope which would sit in the centre of the board.

Molly reached over to the box again and brought out the weapons, placing them on the board ready for the game to start. Edward picked up the little metal dagger and turned it over between his fingers. Edward's mood was temporarily subdued as he thought back to his discovery of the items concealed beneath the floorboards at 78 Wordsworth Close. He wondered if Mr S Thompkins was now behind bars.

'Here's your detective note sheet Dad,' said Becky. 'And a pencil.'

'Have we got any more? The lead's broken in this one. Hang on a minute. There's one on the sideboard in the sitting room. I'll just go and get it.' Edward opened the door to the dark adjoining room, reached round and flicked the useless light switch.

'Oh bugger.'

54

'Mum, could I have some lunch money please?' asked Lizzie one Thursday morning as she and Becky were getting ready for school.

'Lunch money? Why? I gave you a week's worth on Monday,' replied Molly.

'My purse has gone.'

'What do you mean, gone?'

'It was taken on Monday during PE.'

'Oh for goodness sakes, Lizzie. Where did you leave it?'

'In the changing rooms in the pocket of my coat.'

'Why didn't you put it safely in your locker?'

'I forgot it was still in my pocket. I didn't have time to go back to the locker.'

'And this was Monday? How did you buy lunch on Tuesday or yesterday?'

'I didn't have any.'

Mollie was becoming increasingly irritated.

'Why on earth didn't you tell me? I don't know Lizzie, I really don't know. Fetch my purse from the other room and I'll see what I have got in the way of change.'

Lizzie brought her mother's purse into the kitchen handed it to Molly who held in clumsily against her body with her plaster cast clad left arm. She took out sufficient coins for two lunches.

'Here you are. Now please be more careful in future. I can't just hand out money willy nilly because you've been irresponsible. And when you get to school you had better report the stolen purse. I don't suppose you have bothered to do that have you?'

Lizzie was silent.

'No. I didn't think so.'

55

'Let's go down to Eastwater for the day tomorrow,' proposed Edward when another Saturday Night Nosh Night was coming to a close.

'If we got up really early we could be there for 11ish, have a walk, get some lunch, leave again around 5pm and be back here for about 10.30pm I reckon.'

Edward's spontaneity displayed itself from time to time in such propositions. Over the years Molly had become accustomed to them and, in her head, she loosely graded them. At the bottom end of the scale they were whimsical but achievable with a little effort. These low grade ideas were generally worth carrying through as they would provide amusement or some kind of short lived gratification; for Edward, for her, or for the girls. At the other end of the scale were hare-brained suggestions which seemed to have no basis in reality, or no regard for safety, or no consideration of expense. In recent years circumspect Molly often had to try and gently talk her husband out of the 'high level' schemes. In the early days, she just went with it. It was exciting to be in the company of a man who could dream up an exhilarating plan at the drop of a hat and who wanted to enrich their lives with thrilling experiences regardless of the consequences. She remembered the week in France. They were young. Newly wed. Edward was an architectural student, studying hard to gain his qualification but outside of college time he would find paid work to sustain them for the forthcoming term. After one summer break, having earned seventy pounds over the course of several weeks, he spent the entire amount on a surprise trip to Paris and Molly was delighted. They stayed in a beautiful little hotel. Very French with its window shutters, high ceilings and baroque furniture. They strolled hand-in-hand along the Boulevard St-Germain, stopping off at intimate little restaurants or coffee houses, they visited several galleries where they stood in silent admiration of incredible art work, and they took a boat ride along the Seine. So romantic. So perfect. So like Ed to be so kind and considerate. Molly was the luckiest girl alive during those seven days. In the weeks that followed however, when Edward was back in college and she was working as a secretary to a company director, she realised she was having to supress feelings she wished she didn't have. Her Parisian memory was now being tarnished with regret. Trying to find enough money for the rent now or for groceries and then, worst of all, having to go cap in hand to Edward's mother when funds ran out.

As far as Molly was concerned the Eastwater proposal was fairly high on the 'Edward Greenacre's Reckless Ideas Chart.' Definitely in the upper half. Definitely worthy of a 'stupid' label. Ten or eleven hours' driving so that they could spend a maximum of six hours in a county they had turned their back on less than a year earlier. It didn't really make sense. And yet, South Humberside had not delivered much in the way of pleasure for Molly or for the girls, she knew that. Edward would never admit that he didn't care for the place either, but Molly sensed it. Molly knew it. It was an indisputable fact. The south coast sounded very appealing, even for six short hours sandwiched between hours of those six pages of red road again. Before she knew it she was answering in the affirmative and Ed's infectious enthusiasm was taking hold of her too.

'Girls, come down here a minute, would you?' Molly called up the stairs and both daughters emerged from their rooms and followed their mother into the sitting room.

'Daddy and I have made plans to take a trip to Eastwater for the day tomorrow.'

'Made plans' was overstating things somewhat thought Molly. It was more of an impulsive decision, taken rashly without any concept for the intricacies of the notion. 'We're going to need to get up really early, before it's even light. Alright? So I want you to sort out what clothes you're going to need, clean your teeth and get to bed. I'll wake you up in the morning, nice and early.'

'Will we be going to see Judith?' asked Lizzie.

'No, sorry. We won't have time for that tomorrow, but maybe I'll write to Diana and ask if Judith can come up here in the school holidays and stay for a few days.' Molly knew that both girls were missing their friends and, except for Helen, had experienced difficulty establishing friendships in their new schools. Lizzie smiled at the thought of spending time with her old friend, but the school holidays were a long way off.

'Can we get some candy-floss? enquired Becky.

'If we can find some, yes. Now off you go and do as I say. Get your clothes out ready, clean your teeth and get into bed.

Both girls turned and ran back upstairs to do as their mother requested. Molly noticed, as they skipped back to their bedrooms, how their spirits had been lifted. Complying with Ed's crazy idea was perhaps a good decision after all.

56

The following morning at 5.00am, Molly woke the girls and told them they had thirty minutes to have a wash and get dressed. Their initial sleepiness soon gave way to quiet but enthusiastic anticipation for the day ahead. Ed and Molly had already been up for an hour. Ed had got the car out of the garage (as quietly as he could to avoid disturbing the neighbours) and stacked it with all the necessary paraphernalia for their day trip to Eastwater: blankets and spare pillows for the girls, a metal tin containing sandwiches prepared by Molly, thermos flasks full of hot tea, and of course, the road map. Pinky Pig would be stashed at the last minute. When everyone was ready, they got into the car and Ed manoeuvred it quietly down Redridge Close; they turned down the hill to commence their long journey.

Going home. Just for the day, but going home nonetheless. That's what it felt like to each member of the Greenacre family, but none of them admitted that feeling to the others. Home was a place where you felt secure, where you felt at ease, where you had like-minded friends. Home was a good place to be. The town where they resided now afforded none of that comfort. Ed drove steadily through the dark, empty roads, out of that nasty, smelly little town and onwards towards the open countryside. It had rained overnight and both the bright moon and the car headlights lit up puddles in the road ahead. A silver pathway leading tantalisingly toward a place they had missed so much over the last few months. Lizzie and Becky pulled their blankets around their shoulders, laid their heads back onto the pillows and watched the dark fields and trees rush past the car windows. Within a few miles, Becky fell asleep. Lizzie was drowsy but didn't sleep. Her thoughts were running from Judith to her old school, to Eastwater seafront, to her old Girl Guides group and her piano teacher. These memories were interspersed with fleeting teenage imaginings of walking on the beach with David Cassidy. If David Cassidy wasn't going to be in Eastwater today, and thus unavailable, then David Essex would do.

Molly was quiet. She unconsciously stroked her left arm through the sleeve of her winter coat. Newly released from its plaster cast, the skin was tender and tight. The map was on her lap and open on the first page. It was too dark to read but Ed knew this part of their route well enough for it not to matter. Every now and then Molly looked across at the profile of her handsome husband. He was a confident but careful driver. How fortunate I am to be married to this man. This kind, caring, nurturing man. Very slightly eccentric perhaps, but there are far worse traits. Molly loved her husband. She smoothed out the pages of the map and focused her eyes on the silver pathway which Ed was following. Molly wished she didn't have to keep anything secret from him.

57

In Norfolk, at 8am, Phyllis took an important piece of paper from her kitchen drawer. With trembling hands she unfolded it. On it was written, in Molly's handwriting: Colin - Neighbour in Redridge Close. 0724 33165. Phyllis refolded the piece of paper and put it in the pocket of her floral waist apron. She lifted her coat from the hook in the hallway, put it round her shoulders and pushed open the door to the sitting room at the front of the house.

'I won't be long Rose. Keep hold of Dad's hand and I will be back as soon as I can.'

Rose had her chair as close to the makeshift bed as she could get it. She held Reginald's frail bony hand as tight as she dare and looked at the sallow skin on his face. His head was lolling back on to the pillow and his mouth was slightly open. Rose listened to him breathe. It was soft and slow. He had his eyes closed but when Rose spoke to him she could see him trying to open them and respond to her. She wished her sister Molly was with her now. She didn't know what to do to make things better for her mother or father and the inability to do anything constructive made her chest ache.

Pulling her coat on properly now, Phyllis left the house by the back door, opened the wooden side garden gate and crossed the street. A few doors further up was a big, white painted house. Phyllis knew the house and its owner well as she cleaned there twice a week. Did an excellent job too. That's what Mrs Ashbourne said, even though she didn't pay Phyllis particularly well. Phyllis walked along the pathway to the left hand side, went around to the back and knocked on the door. After several seconds, a tall, elegant woman answered.

'Oh hello Phyllis dear. Come in. How's Reg today?'

Phyllis entered the lobby and wiped her shoes on the mat.

'Not so good, I'm afraid, Mrs Ashbourne. May I use your telephone? I need to ring Molly.'

'Of course, you can dear. You know where it is.'

Phyllis walked through to the front hallway, sat down at the telephone table and picked up the receiver. She took the piece of paper from her apron pocket and carefully dialled the number which Molly had written down.

It rang several times before Colin answered.

'Hello. Colin Sanderson speaking.'

'Hello Mr Sanderson. I'm sorry to call you so early on a Sunday, but I need to get a message to my daughter, Molly Greenacre. I believe she's a neighbour of yours. I'm her mother, Phyllis Dean.'

'Ah yes. Hello. Molly did tell me she'd given you my number.'

'Well if you wouldn't mind telling her that I think she needs to get down here as soon as she can. Her father is gravely ill. We're not sure how much ... well, what I mean is, he's taken a turn for the worse ...' her trembling voice trailed off.

'I'm so sorry to hear that Mrs Dean and I will certainly pass on the message. Now, I'm not sure when that will be as they all went out really early this morning at about 5.30am. Funny sort of a time to go out on a Sunday if you ask me, but rest assured that as soon as they are back, I'll go over and pass on your message.'

'Thank you Mr Sanderson. I'm very grateful.'

'Goodbye. And I'm sorry to hear your news.'

'Goodbye. And thank you.' Phyllis replaced the receiver and sat very still for a couple of seconds, wondering why her daughter and son-in-law would have left the house so early. She then tucked the piece of paper back into her apron and walked towards the rear of the house where her employer was waiting discretely by the back door.

'Thank you Mrs Ashbourne. I must get back now.' Phyllis extended her hand in which she had been clasping a 10p coin.

'That's really not necessary Phyllis' said Mrs Ashbourne, wrapping her hands around Phyllis's and gently pushing them away. 'You get back to Reginald now. And don't worry about work tomorrow. You just be where you need to be.'

Phyllis was stoic and not one normally prone to bouts of emotion, of any kind, but her employer's kind words made sharp tears prick unexpectedly at her tired eyes. She fought them back and quickly left the big white house, making her way back along the tree-lined road to her own modest home.

She entered quietly and joined her ailing husband and Rose in the front room.

'I've left a message with Molly and Ed's neighbour. Let's hope she gets it soon.'

Rose looked at her mother's weary face while she was speaking and noticed how she appeared suddenly old. She turned back to her father and, still holding his hand spoke to him softly. 'Dad. Can you hear me? Molly will be here soon. Everything will be alright, Dad. I expect you'll be pleased to see her, won't you?'

Reginald's grip on his youngest daughter's hand tightened very slightly and his eyes opened a tiny bit momentarily. He tried to speak but no words would form.

'Shush Dad. Don't exert yourself. Just lie still and relax. Mum and I are here. We're going to take care of you Dad. Do you want some water?' Rose lifted a glass to her father's lips and supported his head from behind with her left hand. Weakly, Reginald took a small sip. As Rose lowered his head back on to the pillow, a tiny dribble of water fell from the corner of his mouth and ran down his bristly chin. Tenderly Rose wiped it away with a clean cotton embroidered handkerchief.

Unable to directly observe this moment of tenderness between her dying husband and her youngest child, Phyllis busied herself by stacking more coals on the open fire and sweeping the hearth. When she turned around, she could see Rose stroking her father's head gently. She had also begun to hum one of Reginald's favourite hymns but the tempo was too slow and after every few notes, she had to stop and catch her breath. Come on Molly, please hurry up. Please be here. We need you. We all need you. Especially Dad.

58

Page four of the road map now and the dawn had revealed a cold, bright, crisp day. Pools of pale sunshine lava were erupting from behind the South Downs and spilling down the hillsides towards the farm buildings and cattle that had gathered around them ready for milking. As the sun rose higher into the azure sky, a sense of excitement was building inside the vehicle which belonged to the Greenacre family, and which had been expertly piloted by the proud head of that family, Edward. Becky had slept for almost the whole of the first half of the journey but awoke when her father pulled over in Bedfordshire for a 'wee break and a leg-stretch'. Lizzie had drifted in and out of a light sleep but was now completely alert and full of happy anticipation. As they neared their destination, Molly and Edward chatted about the practicalities: where they should park, which restaurants might be open - they were hoping their favourite, The Captain's Table, would be - and where they should walk.

It was just before 11 o'clock when Edward turned right out of a quiet street lined with tall Victorian houses and drove along the seafront. He could see there would be plenty of spaces to choose from at this time on a winter Sunday morning.

'I'll get in at the other end of the seafront, Molly. That way we can walk back this way, turn around at the Big House and then head back for lunch about half one.'

Molly didn't answer, but Edward was confident she would be happy with those arrangements. He drove slowly along the seafront, glancing over occasionally to his left where the beach looked pristine and the sea very blue. White topped waves were breaking on to the sparkling shingle at the water's edge. On his right, on the other side of the road, beyond the central strip of municipal gardens, was a row of elegant hotels and houses. Halfway along the seafront was the pier. As they drove past, Molly looked towards it and it seemed to her like many years had gone by, not just a few months, since she last saw it. A knot in her stomach tightened. Edward had spotted somewhere to leave the car just beyond a kiosk and he pulled into it and turned off the engine. He sat back into his car seat, inhaled deeply and let out a huge satisfying seaside sigh, looking into his rear view mirror where he could see his daughters on the back seat.

'We're here girls! Eastwater! We're going to have such a lovely day! Are you ready?'

'Ready' shouted both girls in unison.

The Greenacres got out of their car. Edward walked around to join his family on the promenade and stood stretching his stiff limbs for a second or two while Molly helped Lizzie and Becky with their coats, hats and gloves. An elderly man walked by with his small terrier dog straining on the lead in front of him. He raised his hat to the family as he passed.

'Good morning. Beautiful day.'

'Good morning to you Sir,' replied Edward. 'It is indeed a lovely bright morning.'

Edward Greenacre was going to forget all about Greythorpe today, with its drabness and stench and more than its fair share of disagreeable people. He was beginning to realise his future did not lie there. It didn't necessarily lie back in the Eastwater area either, but there would be other opportunities for him, which would offer him, and his family, a more contented life. Today he would begin to formulate a plan for the next chapter in their lives. For this one particular day, though, it was all about an Eastwater reminiscence and a bit of escapism. A chance to fill their lungs with sea air and recharge their happiness batteries, which even the upbeat Edward had noticed had been run rather low of late.

'Let's go and see if we can book a table first,' suggested Edward. The family crossed the road and walked down a familiar, and currently empty, small side street towards The Captain's Table. The winter sunlight was catching the very tops of the buildings and reflecting off the top floor windows but down below at pavement level it was in deep shadow and calm and quite cool. Bells were ringing out from a church at the far end of the street. The eleven o'clock congregation were being summoned to their place of worship by the sound of struck brass resonating magnificently in the clean morning air. A nonchalant feline appeared from a doorway and strolled slowly across the road in front of the family as they approached the restaurant. Edward smiled in silent admiration of the cat's aloofness. The restaurant door was locked but inside the Greenacres could see someone setting up tables for lunch. Edward knocked gently on the door to attract the man's attention. The man looked up and smiled, put down his cloth and the handful of cutlery he had been polishing and came towards the door.

'Good morning Sir. Can I help you?'

'We'd like to book at table for lunch please,' said Edward. 'Half past one, if that's convenient.'

'Of course, 4 people at half past one. Name Sir?'

'Greenacre.'

'Look forward to seeing you then.'

'Many thanks,' said Edward and raised his hand to wave a polite goodbye as the man closed the door.

59

Colin got out of his slightly grubby armchair and looked out of his front room window for the seventeenth time that morning. Still not back. No sign of them. Very odd that they should have gone off so early. He would walk up to the paper shop shortly, buy his Sunday papers like he always did, and hope that they had returned by the time he got back. Colin wandered into the kitchen, made himself a mug of tea, stirred in two large spoonfuls of sugar and resumed his post by the front room window. Martin, at number seven opposite, had appeared in his driveway and was wielding a large bucket of soapy water and a sponge. Colin just had time to notice that the car wasn't even particularly dirty before he put down his mug on the windowsill and went across to speak to his neighbour.

'Hello, Martin. Keeping the car all spruced up, I see.'

'Oh. Hello Colin. How's things?' Martin could have done without any intrusion today as he and Glenda were going out shortly. He wished he hadn't added the last two syllables to his greeting. They were somewhat superfluous. Martin was not an impolite or inconsiderate man generally, but Colin did have a habit of going in to far too much detail when responding to enquiries about his well-being and would often add unnecessary embellishments for dramatic effect. Martin couldn't retract that enquiry now but he could start washing down the nearside front wing of his vehicle with energetic purpose and surely to goodness Colin would get the hint.

'Oh you know, struggling on. I was wondering if you knew where Molly and Edward were today? I heard them go off really early this morning and there's been no sign of them since. Molly's mother rang me about eight-ish to say Mr Dean has been taken really poorly. He's in quite a bad way, as far as I can gather. She wanted to let Molly know, obviously.'

Martin stood upright and put down his bucket. 'I'm sorry Colin. We really haven't had that much to do with them yet. They are busy people, as are we. Not been much opportunity yet to get to know them unfortunately so I really don't know about their comings and goings.'

'Well, not to worry Martin. I'll keep an eye out for them and let you get on with washing your car. See you later.'

Martin had conflicting emotions as he watched Colin cross the road back to his home. On the one hand he appreciated Colin had an important message to relay and he felt sorry that he had to shoulder a certain amount of neighbourly responsibility. On the other hand, he was glad it was a short conversation for once and he and Glenda wouldn't be held up getting to their lunch date.

60

'When was the last time Dad ate anything?'

'I made him a sandwich last night but he hardly ate any of it.'

Both women knew that he was getting to the point where he would be unable to eat – the doctor had warned them of that when he called in on them all two days previously – but they both dearly wanted to nurture and care for this much loved man and felt they had to offer something. Rose turned back to her father and took hold of his hand again. 'Dad – can you hear me, Dad? Are you hungry? Would you like anything to eat?'

Reginald managed to slowly shake his head.

'No? Thirsty then? Are you thirsty Dad? Would you like some water?' She held the glass close to her father's lips and again, supported his head from behind with her other hand. Reginald took a tiny sip of water. It seemed like a huge effort to swallow it. Leaning forward again he took another sip and Rose gently lowered his head back into the feather pillow. Phyllis smoothed the eiderdown and blankets and took hold of her husband's hand. It felt warm and soft but the skin was fragile and large green-blue veins stood out on the back. Phyllis noted than his fingernails were still pink. She remembered how her father's fingernails turned blue not long before he died. The image had imprinted itself in Phyllis's mind and made her feel incredibly sad. She had sat with her father, just as Rose was doing now, holding his hands with the blue fingernails, and trying hard, so hard, to be helpful and hopeful. Now here was life's great circle, sweeping them round in its whirlpool, dragging them round while they are trying to reach out for something, anything, to hang on to. Why has Molly not yet called back? Mrs Ashbourne said she would come straight over when she heard anything and there had been no sign of her.

'I'm going out to bring in some more coal for the fire, Rose,' she told her daughter as she picked up the enamel bucket and headed out towards the back yard where the bunker was. 'I'll put the kettle on when I get back.' Phyllis needed to keep busy. The inevitability of the next few days was gnawing at her heart and making her dizzy with fear. She was suppressing the panic by moving around and finding domestic chores to do which didn't really exist or didn't really matter at the moment. She could contain the terror if she kept herself occupied, just like she did in the war years when air raid sirens were wailing and bombs were falling around them in this very street where they still lived. Poor Mr Stanton four doors down. His house took a direct hit. His fingernails never had a chance to turn slowly blue. Alive one minute and dead the next. Earth to earth, ashes to ashes, dust to dust. Come on Molly, call Mrs Ashbourne, will you? Where are you?

61

At the precise moment that her mother was tipping coal into her white enamel bucket, Molly was walking, with Ed and Lizzie and Becky past a wooden bench on Eastwater's main promenade. Ahead they could see the pier, with the white-topped waves breaking and lapping around the supporting legs on the foreshore.

'Mummy, can we go along the pier please?' asked Becky.

'Of course you can. Go on. Run ahead. Daddy and I will catch you up.'

Becky and her sister ran towards the pier entrance. Edward watched his daughters and took hold of his wife's hand. He noticed that she was squeezing it really tightly and interpreted that as an indication that she was as pleased as he was to be out in the sunshine and fresh winter air, walking along a beautiful stretch of coastline and well away from any industrial sulphurous stench. This was a good day. Perhaps a watershed day. A watershed at Eastwater. Edward and Molly quickened their pace and they soon joined their daughters on the pier. They found them walking slowly along the boardwalk, looking down through the gaps to the sea below.

'How far down is the water, Daddy?' asked Becky.

'Oh, I don't know. Quite a drop. Maybe twenty or thirty feet? Changing all the time of course as the tide comes in and goes out again.'

'Would you die if you fell down there?'

'Quite possibly, yes, but let's not think about dying today, shall we?'

Both girls moved on further towards the end of the pier, scattering the seagulls into the air, as they did so. The gulls circled around for several seconds and landed back on the boardwalk again, but this time out of harm's way. Their wing feathers were ruffled by the sea breeze as they moved around the pier on the lookout for anyone who might throw them a crust or a cold chip. Other gulls were lined up on the handrail which went all the way around the pier and one was balanced on the metal telescope which was at the very end of the pier. Lizzie ran towards it, disturbing the seagull again who flew off out over the sea. She climbed up on to the base.

'Daddy – can I have some money to look through this?'

Edward felt in his pocket, pulled out a selection of coins and inserted one into the telescope coin slot.

'Me too Daddy,' said Becky, impatiently. 'I want a go too please.'

'Hang on. Let Lizzie finish. Then it will be your turn.'

'Come on Lizzie. Hurry up. It's my go now.'

'Shut-up Becky. You're putting me off. The coin hasn't run out yet.'

Usually Molly would have reprimanded her eldest daughter for telling the youngest to 'shut-up' but she was distracted – leaning over the handrail and staring down at the water which was splashing noisily against the barnacle covered metal struts. She barely noticed Lizzie's rudeness and by the time it had registered with her, the allotted time had expired and child number one was stepping down from the telescope. Edward lifted Becky up to put in her coin and take her turn.

'It's not very good, Daddy. I can't see much.'

'Well there's not much to see today. Only one boat out there and it's so far away I can only just make it out. Can you see it?'

'No. Put me down now Daddy.' Becky wriggled – her interest in marine magnification had been extinguished already.

The Greenacres walked around the other side of the pier and back towards the promenade, turning right at the end to continue onwards towards The Big House. When the family had lived in the area and walked along this seafront regularly, The Big House (actually Marine Barracks built in the middle of the previous century) was a convenient point at which to turn round and retrace their steps. An easy walk of nearly three miles, making six in total by the time they had returned to their original starting point. Today the promenade was fairly empty, save for the odd dog-walker or people like themselves who were keen to get some exercise and breathe in the salty air. As they walked, the girls would occasionally hop up on to the concrete wall which ran alongside the wide walkway and every now and then jump down on to the shingle beach to pick up interesting pebbles; heart shaped, stripy, shiny, or ones with holes in them.

'Lizzie, I've got a really smooth one here. Look. With an orange stripe going all the way through it.' Becky stood with her back to the wind which was blowing in off the sea. Strands of her long blonde hair were poking out from the hood of her coat and whipping across her face. As Lizzie ran across the shingle towards her sister, Becky held out her hand to show her older sister the latest discovery.

'Keep that one and chuck the brown one away. That one's nicer.'

Becky hurled the brown pebble as far as she could and it landed with a satisfying 'chink' back on to the beach.

'I've found this one. Do you like it?'

Becky examined Lizzie's stone, which was in fact a piece of dark green glass which had been worn completely smooth by decades of pummelling from sea water, sand and other pebbles.

'It's a precious stone,' exclaimed Becky, her eyes widening at the thought that they might have found something of value.

'It fell out of a mermaid's necklace' said Lizzie. 'Come on, let's look for the rest of it.'

The girls giggled and ran further along the beach, their faces rosy in the cold air and their coat pockets bulging with treasure.

Molly watched her eldest daughter. She was a girl who was on the cusp of becoming a young woman. She had reached the stage in her life where her behaviour could switch between being childlike, or that of an adolescent. A difficult age perhaps. Today, though, she was a child. By the time Molly reached Lizzie's age, she had lived through five years of war. In retrospect that seemed terrifying. Molly's own children were so fortunate. Lucky to have us as parents, lucky to live in peacetime with plenty of food on the table and a nice warm, comfortable home. The home, perhaps, is not where we want it to be, but no-one is going to drop a bomb on it. It's safe.

62

Colin looked at the clock which hung on the wall over his mantelpiece. Five thirty-five. He walked over to his sitting room window again. It was dark now and everyone in Redridge Close had their lights on apart from number eleven. Martin and Glenda had been out and come back again and he'd seen Mrs Barrett's daughter arrive and leave again after only half an hour. You'd think she should spend a bit more time with her elderly mother. Really. Half an hour. What good is that? Poor old dear. Ralph Wood at number five had been out with his dog twice today and Beryl Williams had been cutting back her Forsythia in the front garden. Completely the wrong time of year to be doing that. It won't flower now. She has been told it's the wrong time of year but said she doesn't like yellow. Who doesn't like yellow in a garden in springtime? The woman's a bit mad, surely? Where on earth are the Greenacres though? Been out for twelve hours now.

Colin wondered whether to put a note through their door but considered the information he was required to impart too sensitive for that. Besides he knew Molly would be very concerned about her father's condition and would likely be upset. She might need consoling in some way. He sat back down in his chair and turned the television sound down a little to ensure that he would be able to hear any vehicle which came along Redridge Close.

63

'Rose, you go to bed. It's nearly midnight. I'll sit with Dad now. I can sleep in the chair next to him if I have to. I'll wake you if there's any change.'

Reginald's condition hadn't altered much today. He could still hear and make sense of what was being said to him and he appeared to know who it was talking to him. He could respond to questions by shaking or nodding his head or by gently squeezing his wife's or youngest daughter's hand. His eyes had been closed for most of the day but sometimes it looked as though he was trying really hard to open them. His breathing was steady. His skin was warm but his lips were dry. Rose had been applying small amounts of Vaseline to them after she had held up the water glass. His fingernails were still pink. He seemed calm.

Phyllis wondered what he was thinking and hoped he wasn't frightened.

'Alright Mum. I am tired. Thank you. I'll go upstairs but please wake me up if you hear from Molly or if anything here changes.'

Rose leant over and kissed her father on his forehead. 'Goodnight Dad. See you in the morning.' She hoped that she would.

Phyllis heard Rose climbing the stairs and walking around the bedroom upstairs. The floorboards creaked, the bakelite light switch clicked, the metal curtain rings clanked across the curtain pole and the catch on the wardrobe door chinked against its metal stop. Each sound - so regular, so familiar, so ordinary - scratched into the air and hung there. An illustration of normality. But this wasn't normal. This was anything but normal. A union was soon to be dissolved and a new order would have to be established.

Phyllis tried to push thoughts of her upcoming new status to the back of her mind and focussed instead on where Molly might be and how long it would be before she telephoned Mrs Ashbourne to say she was on her way. It would be the morning before she heard anything. At least eight hours probably. Phyllis pulled her chair a little closer to her husband's bed, laid a handknitted woollen blanket across her lap and over her legs, and put her head back and closed her eyes.

64

Edward, Molly, Lizzie and Becky spent a lovely couple of hours in the restaurant and eaten a full three courses at Edward's insistence. The bill was much higher than Molly would have liked, but Ed hadn't batted an eyelid as he paid, and even left a more than adequate tip for their waiter. They had stopped off at The Tree on the way home, a walking area and picnic spot which the Greenacres had visited frequently before moving away. They had set off for home a little later than anticipated and the journey home had been slow due to fog. Finally though they were back. With tired eyes and sinking hearts they pulled up in the driveway of Eleven Redridge Close. It was nearly midnight. Molly took the girls inside straight away and ensured they cleaned their teeth and got into bed. Edward decided he would leave the car on the drive, rather than put it away in the garage. As he was locking up, he was surprised to see Colin, clad in pyjamas and dressing gown, and carrying a torch, walking across the road towards him.

'I need to speak to Molly' said Colin quietly.

Edward was alarmed. 'Well, she's getting the girls to bed. We've had a long day and it's school tomorrow. What's up?'

Colin was finally able to pass on the message he'd been burdened with sixteen hours earlier.

'Thanks Colin. Appreciate you coming across here at this time of night. I'll go and talk to Molly now. Thank you again.' Edward made his way indoors and left Colin to shuffle his way back to Number Three.

65

Mrs Ashbourne's telephone rang just as it was getting light.

'Hello. Mrs Ashbourne? It's Molly here.'

'Hello dear. I was expecting your call.'

'I am so sorry to ring you this early but can you let my mother know that I will get the earliest train down that I can.' Molly was wiping tears from her cheeks with a handkerchief as she spoke.

'Of course. What time do you think you'll arrive?'

'I should be there by midday. Perhaps a little after.'

'I'll go across now and let her know.'

'Thank you. Do you know how my father is?'

'Well, when I spoke to your Mum last night he was quite weak but still able to communicate. He's really poorly, dear. I'm sorry.'

More tears welled in Molly's eyes. 'Okay. Thank you. I'll see you later, I expect.'

Molly replaced the receiver and jumped as she turned around to find Colin right beside her. She felt uncomfortable that he'd seen her crying and didn't like him standing so close to her. Circumstances compelled her to be polite, however.

'Oh. Thanks for use of your telephone Colin.'

'Anytime Molly. Anytime,' and he put his arm round her shoulders. An intrusion which was more than she could bear and she left as quickly as she could.

Edward heard Molly enter the front door and walked through to the hallway where he found his wife distressed and sobbing. He took her in his arms and held her tenderly.

'You spoke to Mrs Asbourne?' he asked her quietly.

Molly nodded.

'Do you know how your Dad is?'

'He's very ill. That's all I know.'

'You go upstairs, pack your bag and I'll take you down to the station. I can get the girls to school.'

Molly went into the bedroom, and shakily pulled a small suitcase from the bottom. She started to fill it with various items of clothing, unsure how much she would need or how long she might be gone. After several minutes the case had been filled with a mismatched assortment of clothes and she closed the metal catches on the front. In the room next door she could hear Edward talking to Lizzie.

'Mummy's got to go off for a day or two and see Grandad. He's not very well. I'm going to be taking her down to the station in a few minutes so that she can catch a train, then I'll come back and take you and Becky to school. Okay? Can you get washed and dressed and help yourself to breakfast? Make sure Becky eats a proper breakfast, can you? Not sponge cake.' Edward smiled a weak smile at Lizzie and she nodded in return.

'Good girl. I'll see you in about three quarters of an hour. I'm just going to wake Becky then Mummy and I will be off to the station.' Edward was always calm in a crisis and was capable of clear and rational thought when a problem presented itself.

66

The train was due to arrive at the changeover point at 10.53am and it would be stopping at five stations en route. Then Molly would have to change trains and there would be a further hour to travel before she would reach her final destination. As her journey progressed, Molly checked her watch, ensuring that they were not running behind schedule. Fortunately neither train was particularly busy so when emotion overcame Molly she could deal with it discretely, wiping her eyes and blowing her nose while looking out of the window and pretending to take note of the changing countryside as it rushed by. It had been several weeks since she saw her father. She had never known him as a completely well man, but then he had been his usual bright and cheerful self, pottering about in his greenhouse, watering plants and potting up cuttings he had taken earlier in the year. That was where he was at his happiest. In his garden, wearing an old donkey jacket and his tatty old work boots and using tools that his own father had passed down to him. Reginald was of the 'make-do-and-mend' generation. He had a shed, as well as the greenhouse. It had been patched up many times when it had fallen victim to extreme weather or just old, deteriorating materials and was now a patchwork of different colours and sizes of wooden panels. Inside it was dark and musty and the shelves were stacked with tins of nails, packets of seeds, coils of wire, balls of string, cans of grease and a whole array of other items required for the maintenance of a small house and garden. Well-worn tools hung from hooks hanging from the shelves and the rafters. Some had their wooden handles secured with screws or bits of old twine. An old kitchen chair in the corner provided Reginald with somewhere to sit if he had felt weak or out of breath (which he often did) or if he wanted to escape from Phyllis, who could often be unfairly 'sharp' with him. As children, Molly, Rose and Gordon would follow him round the garden and in and out of that magical shed. Their father would help them lift the galvanised watering can so they could water the vegetable seedlings or the red geraniums which he grew in great abundance in terracotta pots. There were huge rhubarb plants and tall winding runner bean plants which wrapped themselves around the hazel poles Reginald would secure with rough twine from his shed. A couple of old gnarly apple trees were at the far end of the garden and in the summer their leaves would provide some delightful dappled shade under which Molly and Rose would sit. Daisies and dandelions grew in the grass beneath the trees and the sisters would make long daisy chains and blow the fluffy seed heads of the dandelions into the breeze.

'Not in the direction of my vegetable patch, thank you!' Reginald would call and the girls would laugh then jump up and try to catch the seeds before they hit the ground.

The memories of her father as a younger man flooded into her mind as Molly checked her watch once again. Not much further. How would she find her Dad now? She was scared at the prospect of seeing someone die. It wasn't something she had done before. What if he is scared? How can we comfort him and tell him it will all be alright? Because it won't be alright. I am about to lose my father. Why did we have to go to Eastwater yesterday? My father lay dying and I didn't know. Molly's guilt was overwhelming and she felt herself having to choke back tears again.

Finally the train pulled into the last station. Molly grabbed her case and walked quickly towards the bus stop outside the terminal where she knew a bus could take her the two miles from the city centre up to her old home and where her mother and sister would be waiting for her. Hopefully her father would be waiting for her too.

67

Edward dropped Lizzie and Becky off at the school gates and made his way down through the morning traffic to the town and his workplace. He would be slightly late arriving, but under the circumstances he was sure no-one would mind and this morning's meeting with the contractors wasn't scheduled until 10.00am so he would make it in plenty of time for that. He had always got on extremely well with Reginald and it was a mutually respectful friendship. It was sad that the health problems his father-in-law had suffered over many years appeared to have now got the better of him. As he dropped Molly at the station earlier, she had requested that he call Mrs Ashbourne at about 7pm. It would be easier than Molly calling Colin she said. Edward wasn't entirely sure it would be easier, but he got the sense that those arrangements were important to Molly and so he agreed that he would ring later. He parked the car and went into the offices via the main entrance. He was climbing the stairs to the fourth floor when he met Jennifer, who was on her way down carrying a large box full of files.

'Good morning Jennifer,' said Edward. 'Do you need a hand with that?' Jennifer terrified him but he was a gentleman who couldn't watch her struggle down the stairs with a heavy box.

'Thanks Ed. Very kind of you. Yes please.' She handed the box to Edward.

'Where to?'

'Reception desk please.'

Jennifer was delighted to be on the receiving end of some gentlemanly conduct. It was in rather short supply in this organisation these days, she thought. Edward shuffled the box into a more comfortable carrying position and turned around to walk back down the three flights of stairs up which he had already climbed. Jennifer walked by his side.

'Bit late in this morning,' he explained to Jennifer. 'Sadly my father-in-law has been taken ill and I had to take my wife to the railway station.'

'I'm sorry to hear that Ed.'

'He's been poorly for several years. I've got to make a telephone call tonight to get a progress report and I'm thinking it will probably be bad news.'

'Anyway, how about you? Good weekend?' I shouldn't have asked that, he thought.

'A bit dull, to be honest,' replied Jennifer. 'Not much excitement in my life at the moment.'

'Really? I would have thought you would have been out and about living it up and having fun. What's that new place down near the market where all the young people go? Don't you go there on a Saturday night?'

Edward was really hoping that Jennifer would reply that, yes, she had been there, and with a boyfriend in tow.

'Squires? Well, I would do if I had someone to go with. All my girlfriends seem to be hooked up with lads now and I don't want to go along playing gooseberry.'

'Understandable.'

Edward and Jennifer reached the half landing at the second floor and Marjorie Wilson came through the double doors.

'Morning Marjorie. How are you?' enquired Edward.

'Very well, thank you Mr Greenacre.' Marjorie replied as she stepped around her colleagues to make her way up the stairs. 'I'm off to a meeting with HRH.'

'Right well, don't let us stop you then,' said Edward, smiling.

After descending a further flight of stairs, and when Marjorie was out of earshot, Jennifer whispered to Edward 'She's having a fling with HRH, you know.'

'Surely not?' said Edward who was genuinely shocked by this revelation.

'I swear to God it's true. You seem surprised Edward.'

'Well I am.'

'Don't be,' said Jennifer, pushing open the door to Reception. 'Infidelity is commonplace. Everyone's at it.'

Edward put the box of files down on to a desk. Jennifer smiled at him. A special smile again.

'There's no problem with infidelity, Ed. As long as both parties are happy with the arrangements.'

She turned and walked out of Reception leaving Edward shocked and hoping he would not have to encounter Jennifer again at any time today.

68

Doctor Michaels packed his stethoscope into his large leather bag, stood up and walked through the hallway to the kitchen where Phyllis was peeling potatoes with an old steel knife.

'He's comfortable at the moment, Mrs Dean.'

'Thank you. How long …'

'It's a hard question to answer. But a day at most, I would guess.'

Phyllis put down the knife and felt suddenly weak and shivery.

'Thank you for coming, Dr Michaels.'

'You're welcome. I'll be off now, but call the surgery again if you need me.'

Dr Michaels opened the back door and disappeared round the corner of the house. As he reached his car which was parked in the street, he saw Molly, only a few feet away, running along the pavement towards the house.

'Oh no. Dad. Is he …'

'He's resting at the moment. Your sister is with him.'

'Thank you,' Molly exclaimed breathlessly, as she rushed past and round to the back of the house.

Inside she found Phyllis in the kitchen, filling a large saucepan with water for the potatoes.

'Hello Mum. I'm here at last.

'Hello Molly dear. I can't tell you how pleased I am that you're here.'

'How's Dad doing?'

'Doctor Michaels has said he's comfortable. Rose is with him in the front room. Be quiet. He's asleep at the moment.'

Molly threw her coat over a kitchen chair and, with huge trepidation, entered the front room. Her father looked shockingly thin and old, but thankfully, Molly thought, not distressed in any way.

'Rose. I'm sorry I am so late getting here.' Molly spoke quietly and walked around the other side of the bed, pulling up a chair as close as she could.

'It's alright. Mum and I have been sitting with him for the last couple of days since he took really ill.' Rose was tired and grateful that her sister was now with them.

The room was dimly lit; curtains had been partly pulled across the window to prevent bright light from shining on to the bed. The room was noticeably warmer than the kitchen and hallway as Phyllis had been regularly stoking the fire with coal. Reginald's head was cushioned by a three feather pillows and turned slightly towards one side. His eyes were closed and he was breathing softly; Molly watched the eiderdown rising and falling gently with each breath. He was wearing blue striped cotton pyjamas and his painfully thin arms were outside the bedclothes. On the table beside the bed was a glass of water, an old leather-bound hymn book and his metal framed spectacles which were broken and had been temporarily patched up with sticky tape on one arm. Sadness overcame Molly as she realised he would probably never need to put on those spectacles again. For the last three years, at least, she had teased him about getting a new pair. It was unlikely they would be needed now.

'Do you need a rest Rose? I'll sit with Dad for a bit if you like.'

'Alright. Thank you. I'll fetch you a cup of tea.' Rose was pleased to be relieved from her post for a while. It was emotionally draining and she had felt unable to distract herself from the horror of the situation with chores, like their mother. Rose left the room, pulling the door closed softly behind her.

'Dad. It's me,' Molly whispered, leaning towards her father and gently placing her hand on top of his. 'Can you hear me Dad?'

Reginald stirred and tried to open his eyes. Molly took hold of his bony left hand.

'I've come down on the train Dad. I'm so sorry I wasn't here sooner. I'm here now though.' She felt her father's hand tighten around hers and a huge lump rose in her throat.

'You're not in pain, are you?' Reginald's head moved very slightly.

'It's alright Dad. Don't move. Don't try and speak. Just rest. You don't need to do anything. You don't need to worry about anything.

We're all here. Me, Mum and Rose. We're going to look after you. OK?'

Her voice faltered and large, stinging tears ran down her face. She wiped them away with the back of her hand.

'Ed sends his best, Dad. He's at work today and he took Lizzie and Becky to school this morning. They'll get the bus home later and he will cook their dinner. Goodness knows what that will be. Something easy. It might end up being cheese on toast. I expect he could manage that.'

Molly smiled a joyless smile.

'Are you thirsty Dad? I think we'll get you some nice fresh water in a minute.'

Molly paused for a few seconds but felt the need to continue talking to her father. There might be very few occasions left to do so.

'I saw Doctor Michaels on the way in. He's a good man, isn't he? Still driving round in that funny old car. I think it's almost as old as he is. They sort of go together, don't they? Very good of him to call and check on you.'

Molly looked at Reginald's thin face and realised he was drifting back to sleep so she leaned back in her chair and gently released her father's hand back on to the eiderdown. She sat unmoving for a several seconds, feeling suddenly exhausted and frightened, and then picked up the hymn book. A cross-stich bookmark which Rose had made as a child had been placed somewhere near the middle of the book. Molly opened it, let the bookmark fall into her lap and saw that it had been marking pages on which appeared 'Abide with Me.'

Abide with me; fast falls the eventide;
The darkness deepens; Lord with me abide.
When other helpers fail and comforts flee,
Help of the helpless, O abide with me.
Swift to its close ebbs out life's little day;
Earth's joys grow dim; its glories pass away;
Change and decay in all around I see;
O Thou who changest not, abide with me

Earth's joys had certainly grown dim of late for Molly, but still she had much to be thankful for, she realised that. Molly turned to the very front of the book and saw inside the front cover, written in neat copperplate handwriting, an inscription dated 5th May 1913:

Presented to Reginald William Dean by St Peter's Congregational Church on the occasion of his confirmation.

You were fifteen years old then, Dad, thought Molly. Could you have imagined yourself like this now?

Sixty years had gone by and Dad had grown, lived, loved, been loved and was now nearing the end of his days on this earth. At fifteen he was tall, strong and looking forward to his future as an adult. Since then he had lived through two world wars, brought three children into the world, worked hard, made friends and tended that garden as though it was the most precious piece of land on earth. He'd walked up life's steep hill and was now almost down on the other side. Perhaps it's a good thing that no-one can see what's at the bottom of the hill while we're climbing up towards the summit. We just climb, hope that a beautiful vista stretches out before us when we reach the top and expect a nice easy walk down again. Anyone would want to reach the bottom without stumbling against a rock or falling into a ravine. Dad had descended with obstacles in his way, but he held fast, never complaining about the detours he had to take or how much effort it was to carry on towards his final resting place.

Phyllis entered the room with a cup of tea for Molly.

'Here you are Molly. Rose has made you some tea.'

Molly gratefully accepted the cup and saucer and watched her mother sit down in the little armchair on the other side of Reginald's bed. She looks so tired and sad, thought Molly. If only I could make it better for you somehow. I wonder if you have regrets about your life with Dad. It's been a hard life and I can see that. Sometimes you've taken your resentment out on Dad, even though nothing that has caused you trauma in your life has been his fault: the frightfulness of war, Dad's ill health and my brother's death. And then there's that other thing. That thing we have never spoken about and which has caused you, and I, to keep secrets from each other and those we love.

69

A bell signifying the end of the physics lesson rang and Lizzie picked up her books and shoved them back into her satchel. The next, and final, lesson was English and she was required to descend to the ground floor and make her way to the classroom next to the main entrance. She didn't much care for physics, but English would be better as her friend Helen was in the same group and they sat next to each other. It was the usual squash of pupils on the staircase. Some coming up, whilst others were going down. Weaving past each other like snakes writhing in a bucket. A frenetic flurry of activity for about three minutes until everyone had navigated their way to their next classrooms. Lizzie sat down in her usual spot and Helen soon joined her.

'Did you get your homework done?' Helen asked.

'Yes. Only last night though. But it's finished, thank goodness.'

Lizzie wouldn't normally leave the completion of homework until so late, but her mother was still away in Norfolk and Edward was far from the disciplinarian. Besides, he had other things to think about.

'How many pages did you write?'

'Three and a bit. Do you think that's enough?'

'Yeah, course. I did big writing so it just about filled three pages,' Helen giggled.

'We should be alright then.' Lizzie was relieved.

'I think I saw your Dad last night after school,' said Helen. 'Coming out of the florists on the High Street. Oh, and guess who else I saw? Matthew. THE Matthew. YOUR Matthew? Come on Lizzie, you know who I mean.'

Lizzie blushed. She knew THE Matthew had taken a shine to her, but she was far too shy to respond in any way to his hormonal adolescent advances. Her pretence of not knowing to whom Helen was referring was betrayed by her red face.

Mr Bell, their English teacher entered the classroom.

'Right everyone. Quiet please and eyes front. Paul Richardson. Yes you. This desk at the front please where I can see you.' Paul Richardson sullenly picked up his satchel and slunk to the front of the class where he slumped down in the seat right in front of Mr Bell. As Mr Bell turned away to pick up his copy of 'King Lear', his lesson notes and a biro, Paul Richardson took the chewing gum from his mouth and stuck it to the underside of the desk.

Mr Bell opened the book and perched on the front of his desk facing his pupils. 'Right then. Good afternoon everyone. King Lear. Act Three. What do know so far about Cordelia and her actions with regards to her father? Let's recap. Right from the start. Come on. Anyone want to kick this off? Good – Jane C – what can you tell me about Cordelia?'

'She's the youngest daughter of the King, Sir. There were three of them.'

'Good start,' said Mr Bell, putting down the book and walking around the back of the desk to the blackboard. He picked up the biggest piece of chalk he could find and wrote at the top of the board 'Youngest of three daughters' Turning around to face the class again he continued, 'What else? Come on please. Remember, back in Act One, the King asks all three of his daughters an important question. Act One people. I will remind you that it was only last week we were talking about it. Surely you lot with your young fertile minds haven't forgotten already?' Mr Bell's voice was getting louder. 'WHAT DID THE KING ASK HIS DAUGHTERS?'

Paul Richardson raised his hand. 'He wanted to know if they wanted sausage and chips for tea Sir.'

The class sniggered.

'Pipe down Richardson. A bit more effort with your studies and a lot less at trying to be funny please.'

Fortunately for Mr Bell, Angela Wade was indicating that she had a more appropriate response. 'Yes, Angela. What can you tell me about Lear's kingdom rather than his daughters' culinary requirements?'

'He wanted to know if his daughters really loved him, Sir'

'Good. How much did they love him? Who loved him most? He wanted answers to those questions so that the kingdom could be divided up in accordance with their declarations of love. So tell me, people, was it Cordelia with the greatest declaration?'

'No Sir, shouted out Paul Richardson. 'The other two greedy ones. They reckoned they loved the old boy most.'

Mr Bell was rather impressed with his naughtiest student's appraisal of the plot, although he considered that he could have chosen more suitable language.

'Hand up first please Richardson. And why then, do you think, did Cordelia not declare her love as her sisters did?'

'She wanted fish not sausages.'

Louder sniggering this time.

'SETTLE DOWN EVERYONE. Paula Gibbons. I see you have your hand up. Can you give me a sensible answer please?'

'She doesn't want to flatter her father. It's a kind of game she doesn't want to play, Sir.'

'Excellent, Paula. That's a very mature and well considered answer. Do you think it could be because she might be a bit stubborn too?

'Or shy Sir,' ventured Jane E.

'In what way Jane?'

'Perhaps she was embarrassed to say that in front of everyone.'

'Good point,' said Mr Bell, turning his back to the class once more and writing 'Would not declare love for Lear: No flattery or game-playing. Too stubborn or shy?'

'Turning back again to his pupils Mr Bell asked 'What about integrity? Could it be that, in fact, unlike her sisters, she has integrity? Who can give me a definition of integrity?

Unfortunately the only hand raised belonged to Paul Richardson.

'Yes Paul. Enlighten us with your knowledge of the meaning of integrity.'

'It's when you get sand between your toes on the beach.'

'THAT'S ENOUGH NOW. Right class, thanks to Richardson here you are all going to be set an extra piece of homework tonight. Look up the word integrity in the dictionary and I want a full definition written down, together with a sentence containing the word in its proper context.'

The class groaned in unison.

'Let's move on to what happens to Cordelia after she refuses to play ball. Who can give me an answer, an intelligent answer, about the consequences of her actions? Tim Bateman. We've not heard much from you yet. Can you tell me the outcome for Cordelia when she refuses to comply with her father's request?'

'She gets booted out Sir. And then goes off to marry some French bloke.'

'Well done Bateman. A little less eloquent than I was expecting from you, but you've got the general idea.' And turning round to the board again, he wrote: Banished from Kingdom. Marries King of France. Mr Bell put down the chalk and faced his class again.

'What I would like you all to do now is read through the first four scenes of Act Three. Try and decipher the text into modern day language. How would it be worded if we were speaking now? Now, in 1974. Make notes in pencil please. Rather than a word by word translation, try and get a sense of what Shakespeare wrote and summarise it. Then we'll go through it bit by bit until we can all make sense of it. Think about the language we've looked at already in the first two Acts and apply the same rules. Look closely at the parts where the daughters are mentioned. Try and UNDERSTAND Lear and his reactions to his daughters' treatment of him. Richardson – how many scenes have I asked you to look at?'

'Four, Sir.'

'Good. Four scenes everyone. Off you go and no talking please. You will have ample opportunity to discuss at the end. Don't worry if there are parts which seem indecipherable – we will go through it all together as a class later. You can look up any unknown words if you need to. Do the best you can please.'

The class, as instructed, began to interpret Act Three as best they could, scribbling their notes in pencil where they felt they had understood the text and checking unfamiliar words in their dictionaries. Mr Bell sat down behind his desk and looked up from time to time when he felt the whispering needed to be kept in check. He had in front of him thirty forms in connection with a school trip to Stratford Upon Avon. Moira in the School Administration Office had typed them out for him earlier. He placed each form in an envelope, sealed it and addressed it to the parents of each child in his class. When the buzz in the classroom signified the end of concentration on translating Act Three, Mr Bell stood up and spoke once more to his pupils.

'Alright class. Pencils down for now. Before we start looking at what you've discovered about those first four scenes, I want to talk to you about a trip the school is running to Stratford Upon Avon. Can anyone tell me what's so special about Stratford?'

'It's where Shakespeare was born, Sir' shouted out Kevin Fraser from the back of the class.

'Excellent, Kevin. We're running a trip next month on the Fifteenth. It will be a joint trip. You and Class 3F. It will be a long day - an early start – around 7.00am, returning back to school about 9.00pm. We'll be seeing a production of King Lear while we're there so I would urge you all to attend if you can. All the details are in these letters which you will take home with you this evening please.' Mr Bell held the forms aloft. Lizzie and Helen looked at each other and smiled as Mr Bell informed them of the trip. They were both certain they would have a great day out.

'Now ... Act Three Scene One. We've got Kent and a Gentleman out on the heath. The weather, in Kent's words is foul. It's awful. Imagine the wind howling and the rain lashing down. Why do you think Shakespeare would have his characters out on the heath in such awful conditions? What is he trying to show us?'

'That they missed their bus, Sir?'

'RICHARDSON. If you want to be excluded from the trip, you are going the right way about it. Now please, will someone give me the correct answer?'

The class managed to work their way through the rest of Scene One and were half way through Scene Two when the final bell of the day sounded.

'Well done everyone. We will carry on next time. Thank you all for your attendance. Collect your Stratford trip letter from the desk as you leave. Richardson – stay behind please. You know the drill by now.'

Lizzie and Helen made their way out of the classroom, along the noisy crowded corridor, out through the main doors and into the late afternoon sunshine.

70

Rose was sitting by her father's side. Just as she had for most of the last three days. Holding his hand, stroking his forehead, talking softly to him and listening to his breathing. In the last four hours he had been too weak to accept the sips of water Rose had been offering and now she detected a change in him. His breaths were faster and the colour of his skin was less pink. She briefly left the room and called through to the kitchen. 'Mum, Molly. Do you want to come here?'

'I'm just getting this floor washed,' said Phyllis.

'I'd leave the floor and come through if I were you, Mum.'

Sensing the urgency, Phyllis quickly leaned the mop against the larder door and joined her youngest daughter in the front room. Molly followed and pulled up another chair by the side of hers. All three women sat watching Reginald. Watching his every breath in and out, watching his face. Saying nothing to each other but talking gently to this man who had been a dominant feature in all their lives. In different, but equally loving ways.

'It's alright Dad, we're here.'

'Yes, we're here for you Dad. Don't worry.'

'Everything is alright Reg. Everything is alright.'

'I've got your hand, Dad. Can you feel it? Can you squeeze it?'

Reginald could no longer squeeze his youngest daughter's hand and Rose was too scared to cry.

'We love you Reg. We love you so much,' said Phyllis, sensing the sadness in Rose's voice.

Neither Molly nor Rose had ever heard their mother address their father before in that way. But the gravity of the situation lessened the shock they might otherwise have felt at hearing Phyllis utter those words. It gave them permission to also openly admit their love for their father.

'Yes,' confirmed Molly. 'We love you Dad.'

'So much Dad,' said Rose. 'You're the best father anyone could have. We love you.'

Reginald's breathing began to slow down. Then slower still. Then just one small breath every few seconds. Then one big deep breath and he fell silent. Forever.

71

Molly returned home two days after Reginald had passed away. She had been with Phyllis and Rose to register the death and spoken to the undertakers and the vicar. The three women were shaken and subdued. It was agreed that Rose would stay on with her mother until the funeral and Molly would return with Edward in two weeks' time.

When Molly had spoken to Ed on Colin's telephone to break the news, Edward was extremely sad. His own father had passed away when Ed was just twenty-eight. Richard Greenacre had fought in the first world war and although he was 'lucky' to return home, he lived with the effects of mustard gas for the rest of his life. Those effects finally claimed him when he was fifty-six years of age. From the minute that Edward had met Reginald, soon after the courtship with Molly commenced, the two men formed a strong bond and a mutually respectful friendship. They became closer still after Richard's death. Reginald and his son-in-law were two very different men, but they shared a lot of admirable characteristics and a naughty sense of humour. When they had a chance to get together they would sit chatting until the early hours - long after Phyllis and Molly had gone to bed - drinking whisky and mulling over a variety of subjects. Reginald in his own quiet, calm and caring way had been a huge support to Edward after Richard Greenacre's death. Similarly, Edward had helped Reginald when and where he could. Often in practical ways as Reginald's health deteriorated. Over the last few years, Edward had fixed new glass in his greenhouse after a storm, installed an outside tap for him to use in the garden and carried out many other household repairs with which Reginald would have struggled. Painful arthritic fingers and the cruel symptoms of a degenerative condition made many household tasks impossible.

Edward broke the news to Lizzie and Becky the morning following that telephone call from Molly. The girls took the information in their stride and Edward assessed them as being sufficiently calm to go to school. In reality, because they had never been geographically close to their grandfather, and had therefore only ever seen him for a few days at a time during the occasional visit in school holidays, they didn't feel bereft like their mother or father. They had always enjoyed Reginald's company as he was a genial and generous Grandad, but the truth was they hadn't really ever spent much time with him.

Edward took the girls to school and picked up Molly from the station in Greythorpe later in the day. A gentleman as ever, he took her suitcase from her as she stepped down from the train and opened the car door for her when they reached the station car park.

'He didn't suffer, in the end, did he Molly? Please tell me he passed peacefully away without any pain.'

'No Ed. He wasn't in pain. It was just a gentle step across that final line. We were holding his hand and talking to him and it was all very ... dignified. It was how it should be.'

'And how's your Mum been?'

'She's alright. She's strong Ed. She will be sad, but she will cope. It's Rose I am more worried about. She's putting on a brave face for Mum's sake but it's going to be really difficult for her.'

Edward started the car and they drove home in silence, each reflecting on their own relationship with Reginald and how the world had now changed for them both.

Molly walked through the front door and it felt like she had been away much longer than just a few days. Everything looked the same but felt different. The armchair seemed empty, although bizarrely Reginald and Phyllis had never visited this house. Molly couldn't understand why she had that feeling. The wall clock was ticking but its tick seemed louder and more insistent. The view along Redridge Close from the sitting room looked bleaker than she remembered. She could just see Colin's house near the far end by the junction. She would have to face the unpleasant task of visiting him tomorrow to thank him for use of his telephone. As much as she hated to admit it, he had been a huge help in relaying messages and allowing her to keep Edward informed of what was going on. She tried to put the thought of a visit to the back of her mind and went into the kitchen.

Edward took Molly's case upstairs and laid it on the bed ready for unpacking, then knocked on Lizzie's and Becky's bedroom doors where they were both doing homework – or that's what they had told Edward anyway.

'Mummy's home. She's downstairs. Are you going to come down and help her get dinner ready?' It was more of a polite command than a suggestion.

The girls went down to the kitchen and were each given their respective mealtime duties. Becky set the table, enlisting help from her father when it came to deciding which way round the cutlery should go, and Lizzie was charged with peeling carrots and potatoes.

'There's a letter from the school about a trip next month,' said Lizzie to her mother as she flung a badly peeled potato into a large aluminium pan of water. I left it on the worktop. Did you see it?'

'Yes, I saw it Lizzie. I'll take a look at it later.'

'We've got to get it back to Mr Bell by Friday.'

'Alright. Well, as I said, I'll read it later. Now, how many potatoes have you done? We're going to need six medium sized ones I think.' Subconsciously, Molly was taking a leaf out of Phyllis' book. Take on domestic trivialities to keep oneself from being consumed by thoughts and memories which sometimes, for sanity's sake, had to be pushed to one side.

72

Edward walked along the corridor from his office to that of the Department Manager having been summoned there earlier in the day. He checked his watch which read 4.30pm. Bang on time, just as he liked it. He knocked on the door of Jennifer's office and entered when he heard her answer.

'Hello Ed. How lovely to see you,' she smiled that smile again.

'Mr Jameson is ready for you. You can go on through.'

Mr Jameson was indeed ready and he opened his adjoining office door to greet Ed.

'Good afternoon, Edward. Come in please. Take a seat.'

'Thank you Sir,' said Edward as he sat down in the chair opposite Mr Jameson's desk.

'How are you?' asked Jameson as he gathered up the papers he had been looking at earlier, placed them inside a cardboard folder and put them to one side.

'Very well, thank you.'

'Excellent. Well, it won't come as any surprise to you to know that the reason I've asked you here today is to discuss your contract. You've been here now, what, eleven months?'

'Yes, about that.'

'Well you'll be aware that your twelve month contract will be coming to end in March, although of course you will recall that at your interview we discussed the likelihood of it being extended for a further year.'

'That's right Sir, we did,' replied Edward.

Jameson picked up a document from a metal tray on the side of his desk and put on his reading glasses to study it. 'You've been working on the Gately Estate project with Michael Mayhew and that is now nearing a successful conclusion, due, in no small part to your efforts. How have you found the process Edward?' asked Jameson, looking up from the document over the top of his spectacles.

'I've enjoyed it in the main,' replied Edward. 'We've had our ups and downs but principally I think it's been a great success. The only real problems have come from tenants not wanting to co-operate, but in the end Michael and I managed to convince them that what we're trying to achieve is for their benefit, so they have come round ultimately. The contractors have done a good job and it's been a pleasure working alongside them. Yes, all in all, I would say it's gone well.'

'Well, we've now had confirmation of the next area for improvement assigned under GIA,' said Jameson. 'And the reason I have asked you here today is that I would like you to take on overall control of the new area which will start in April. It will of course mean a promotion for you and all the benefits that that implies.'

'Thank you Sir,' said Edward, delighted that his dedication to his work had been recognised and was now being rewarded.

'I'd like you to have a think about it and give me your decision after the weekend. Here's some information which should be of interest to you,' said Jameson, picking up several sheets of paper from his desk which he stapled together in the top left hand corner and then handed to Edward. 'Details of the contract, budgets, timescales and a full list of the areas you will be responsible for. On the last page is payscale and superannuation data pertaining to this grade and other details specific to the role. We'll talk again on Monday at 4pm if that's alright with you.' Jameson stood up and walked towards the door. Edward followed, paused briefly in the doorway and offered his hand to Jameson.

'Have a good weekend, Edward,' said Jameson, shaking Edward's extended hand warmly.

'You too Sir. Thank you.'

73

Reginald's funeral had been a fitting farewell to a wonderful gentleman. Everyone agreed. Molly and Edward had travelled down to Norfolk to attend and now, the following day, had arranged to drive back to Greythorpe, getting back there around 5.30pm to collect the girls from Helen's. Sylvia Burrows had been very sympathetic when she heard the news and offered to have both Lizzie and Becky to stay for the two days Molly and Ed were away. Molly gratefully accepted Sylvia's kind offer - she and Ed had discussed whether or not to include the girls at the funeral but decided that for both practical and emotional reasons, they would be best staying behind.

Edward suggested taking a walk before they set off on the drive home and Molly agreed it would be a good idea. They needed to clear their heads after the previous day and some exercise wouldn't go amiss either. They broached the subject with Phyllis who was busy sorting out and cleaning the shelves in the larder. She wouldn't join them but was happy for them to go.

'We'll be about an hour I expect Phyllis. See you later,' said Edward as he gently closed the back door and joined Molly who was already standing by the pavement at the front of the house.

'Where shall we go?' Ed asked his wife. 'Is there anywhere in particular you want to walk?'

'Let's just head towards the city, shall we?'

Molly slipped her arm through Ed's and they set off along the footpath through the avenue of chestnut trees which lined the street on both sides. They passed the spot where Mr Stanton with the pink fingernails had met his demise thirty years earlier. The house was rebuilt soon after the end of the war and now it was lived in by a young family. There was no trace of the former horror. Lace curtains where once there was smashed glass and a bank of cornflowers, nasturtiums and poppies in the front garden had replaced the smoking piles of brick rubble and broken roof tiles. At the end of the road Molly and Edward turned right into a wider road, still lined with trees but with grander houses – getting grander as they neared the city centre. As they walked they shared fond memories of Reginald, and because he'd been such a positive force in their lives, they were able to talk about him without becoming overly upset.

'I can see the look on his face now, Molly. He was beaming when I asked him if I could marry you. He was so happy. And then, can you remember him walking you down the aisle? Quite shaky on his feet but determined to do it. So proud he was. So proud.'

Molly could still remember, as they travelled the length of that aisle together towards the smiling Reverend Hartman, how her father's arm felt. Thin, even then, and trembling but she felt utterly secure in his love for her. Now, as Molly was walking along these tree lined streets two decades later she was holding Ed's arm. It felt physically much stronger, and protective. Again she had an overwhelming feeling of security.

'And the bean poles! I don't think I will ever forget how he teased me relentlessly about putting up the bean poles for his runner beans. He didn't know how a half hour job stringing together some old hazel branches could have taken me all afternoon. But I wanted to get it right. All perfectly spaced in the vegetable plot and all neatly tied up with no messy ends flapping about. Your Dad reckoned the beans were going to taste better than they ever had due to my diligence in bean pole handling! The best runner beans this side of Covent Garden he said.'

Molly smiled. 'What about the cabbages? Can you remember that one huge cabbage which was so heavy Lizzie couldn't even lift it?'

'It would have quite easily fed a family of ten for a week.' Ed laughed. 'Didn't I take a photograph of it? Where did that go?'

'It's in an album with some other photos of that summer. There's a couple of Dad in the garden, grinning, fork or spade in hand and standing next to a pile of other gargantuan vegetables.' Molly smiled again at the memory.

'When you think about it now, that was quite a feat, wasn't it?' said Ed. 'I mean his illness was affecting him considerably, even back then, but on his good days he still managed to work in the garden and grow all that lovely stuff.'

'Determined,' replied Molly 'and unfailingly cheerful. That was my Dad.'

The couple walked on in silence for several seconds before another memory bounced into Molly's brain.

'That summer, Ed, that was the one where the girls were asking Grandad to draw pictures for them. Poor Grandad. His hands were shaky and all the pictures looked the same. *That horse looks like a sheep Grandad! Draw me a dog. The dog looks like a sheep too!* Everything looked like a woolly sheep because he couldn't control the pencil.'

'Oh Molly, that's cruel.'

'No. It wasn't cruel,' said Molly gently. 'The children were young and there was no malicious intent on their part. And Dad took it in the spirit it was intended. He wasn't offended. Not in any way. He was just enjoying the company of his granddaughters.'

'You're right Molly. Your Dad had a huge heart, didn't he?'

To stop herself from crying, Molly tightened her grip on Ed's arm and the couple continued their walk without further conversation until they reached the city centre. The vibrant market place was surrounded by elegant buildings on three sides. On the remaining side was the 1930s built City Hall where Edward and Molly had worked and first met.

'How about if we walk to the end of the market, turn up Castle Street and make our way back through the park?' asked Edward.

'Alright. Then we can stop at the bakers and pick up a loaf of bread for Mum.'

Edward was glancing to his left as they were making plans for the second half of their walk. He looked up at his old office window on the first floor and it felt like such a short time ago he was working there. He did a quick calculation in his head. Twenty six years. Twenty six years ago he was there, sitting at his desk, drawing up architectural plans which played their part in the post war regeneration of this city. Twenty six years ago he would stand in that window at 5pm, watching a beautiful young girl on her bicycle, pedalling home at the end of the day. Golden hair streaming out behind her as she freewheeled down the hill, round the corner and out of sight.

74

The final bell sounded exactly at 3.40pm. Class 3C rose to their feet, scraping their chair legs noisily across the classroom floor as they did so.

'Books here on my desk as you go out please,' said Mr Williams loudly.

'And collect a homework sheet as well. I want the homework completed and handed in by Friday. That's Friday this week, not the following Friday or the one after that. No excuses, you understand? Friday.'

Lizzie and her classmates jostled around Mr William's desk, flinging the books down and collecting the dreaded homework sheet. Lizzie stuffed the sheet into her satchel and made her way out of the classroom into the busy corridor. The block of lockers and the cloakrooms, where Lizzie was now headed, were on the floor below. She reached the staircase and a throng of pupils was pushing its way down towards freedom. Lizzie squeezed in with the crowd and began to descend the stairs. Halfway down, and standing still on the side of the stairs, were two girls, one of whom was the pupil who had been on the receiving end of the 'Leave My Sister Alone' incident. Lizzie had made eye contact with her before she realised what was happening and noticed the girl was smiling at her. But it was not a kind smile; Lizzie was astute enough to realise it was a hostile countenance. She immediately averted her gaze as her heart began pounding in her chest. She didn't want to pass the girls but, being squashed in between so many others, meant turning back was impossible. As she drew level, she turned her face away from them and focused on the corridor below but heard them sniggering as she passed. Relieved to have made it to the ground floor she turned right towards the cloakroom and was able to quicken her pace. As quickly as she could she retrieved her bag from her locker and then moved to the opposite side of the corridor to collect her coat from the cloakroom. The coat had been a Christmas gift from her paternal Grandmother. It was made of faux suede and had a faux fur trim around the collar, bottom edge and cuffs. Edward's mother was always very generous with birthday and Christmas presents and loved to lavish expensive treats on her granddaughters, much to the annoyance of her daughter-in-law. Lizzie had been delighted with the coat and begged Molly to let her wear it to school. It was so much nicer, and warmer, than the gabardine mac which she had been wearing last term. Molly relented as she was feeling unwell from a recent bout of tonsillitis and didn't have the strength to argue. So, having been granted permission, Lizzie had been wearing her new coat since the start of term and it had kept her warm on the bus journey to and from school in the bitterly cold winter weather.

But today, as Lizzie lifted the coat off the hook, she was horrified to realise it had been slashed on both the front and the back with something very sharp. There were four long cuts on the front, three more on the back and the lining was showing through the incisions on the main fabric. Lizzie tried to hold back the tears which immediately sprang to her eyes and she trembled as she examined the damage and then shoved the coat into her bag. Her mother was going to be so angry with her when she got home.

75

Early the following morning Edward and Molly were in the living room of 11 Redridge Close, as usual, to have their first drinks of the day and their customary chat.

'Here's your coffee,' Molly said as she handed her husband a cup and saucer.

'Thank you my sweet.'

Edward placed his coffee on the table beside his chair and stirred it slowly.

'Did you sleep well?' he asked.

'Not really. How about you?'

'I must admit, I have been quite restless.' Edward picked up his coffee and blew gently across the top.

'This coat business is very alarming', said Molly. 'Why would anyone do that? And how come pupils are carrying sharp objects around in school?'

'I'm shocked. Totally shocked. And I know Lizzie doesn't want us reporting the matter to the school, but we'll have to. We can't just let this drop. Someone is responsible for doing such an awful thing.'

'We'll have to replace the coat. That's an expense we could do without,' said Molly. 'I've explained to Lizzie that there'll be no school trip now. We can't afford to pay for that and a new coat.'

Edward and Molly sat in silence for a few minutes, drinking their coffee and both feeling miserable and disappointed.

'You know Molly, Norfolk is a lovely place, don't you think?'

Molly knew instinctively what Edward was about to propose.

'I feel it's my home, Ed. It's where I grew up. It's where we met.'

Molly put down her empty coffee cup on the table beside her.

'Graham and Suzanne have settled in well there too,' she said. 'And we did have a nice time there when we went to visit them at Easter.'

Molly found herself already sanctioning what she knew Ed was about to suggest.

'I'm considering a move back there for us,' said Edward. 'There would be lots of advantages. We would be close to the coast again, the pace of life would be a bit less frantic and of course we mustn't forget your mother or mine. Neither of them is getting any younger and it would be good to be nearer to them. They're probably going to need our help sooner or later. Graham has said there is no shortage of architectural work in his practice so I know I could easily find work. Let's be honest. This place hasn't really lived up to our expectations, has it? We could find a nice house, maybe in the countryside, and perhaps one which we could 'do up'. I would like to have another project. Hambleton Cottage was a huge success wasn't it? I could do that again. In fact, I would relish the idea.'

'It's worth thinking about I suppose,' said Molly, trying hard to supress the trepidation that she was feeling. 'And you did make an excellent job of doing up Hambleton Cottage.'

Whilst providing her husband with the answer she felt duty bound to give, and that he had come to expect, Molly was well aware that Edward had spent his restless night stacking up the potential benefits to support his argument. In just a few seconds he had listed several; the proximity to the coast, the escape from a constantly busy environment, the mothers, the work and the opportunity to renovate a property in the countryside. All of those advantages were appealing to Molly (apart, perhaps, from being closer to her mother-in-law) and yet at the same time she knew it would mean another wrench away from familiarity. They had been in Greythorpe for less than a year, and despite several unsavoury and unfortunate events, she was beginning to feel settled. She had made a good friend in Sylvia, was about to join the local Womens' Institute and she had worked hard at getting their home and garden in order.

'What about the promotion though? You've worked so hard Ed.'

'Blow that. It's only work. I am going to call Graham this evening,' said Edward. 'Let's see if we can get back down there for a couple of days while we house hunt. And I'll also ring a few of the estate agents in the area to see if they will post us some particulars of property for sale that would be possible viewings. A fresh start, that's what's needed.'

The 'fresh start' concept was beginning to feel a bit stale as far as Molly was concerned. They had already endured several and they had only been living at Redridge Close since last summer. And while she was well aware that Humberside had been a difficult transition after the south coast, the idea of having to re-pack all their belongings and relocate to yet another unfamiliar area was daunting. What if it was a case of out of the frying pan into the fire? She would not voice those reservations to her husband, however.

76

Within a couple of days a pile of estate agents particulars, which were the result of Edward's impulsiveness, was stacked neatly on the coffee table in the sitting room.

'Take a look at these Molly.' Edward was bright and full of enthusiasm for the upcoming changes which, in his mind, were already on track and would come to fruition by the end of the spring. 'I've put the best ones on top and those I am not completely sure about underneath. They still might be worth a look though. You can't really tell until you see the place.'

Molly picked up the pile of papers and looked through them. There were several modern semi-detached houses on small housing estates near towns, a couple of 1930's houses in need of improvement, a cottage in a remote hamlet with a river running across the end of the garden and a run-down red brick Victorian cottage in a quiet village.

'Quite an interesting selection Ed.'

'I think there's enough choice for starters. I just told the agents to send me anything in our price bracket and with at least three bedrooms in the area we are looking at. Anything that isn't on a main road and has a decent sized garden. Graham's calling back this evening to let us know if they can put us up next weekend. If so, we will head down on Friday afternoon to make the most of the available time. Oh, and I called into Hotsons yesterday on my lunch break and they are sending round a valuer tomorrow with a view to getting this place on the market. We'll stick with them, I think. They were pretty good when we bought through them and they know the house, so I don't think it's worth wasting time looking round for other agents. Will you be here tomorrow at lunchtime?'

'Yes, I should be here,' said Molly.

'I'll pop home from work so that I'm here too when the chap calls. They said it would be about one-ish.'

77

Precisely at one o'clock the following day, Eric Hotson knocked on the door of 11 Redridge Close.

'Good afternoon, Mr Hotson. Please come in, do.' Edward shook his hand and took him through to the sitting room.

'Well. This is a pretty quick turnaround. I think it was July when you completed on the purchase, wasn't it?' The agent was scanning the room as he spoke. Nothing too major in the way of changes since he last sold this house, save for the personal possessions of the Greenacres. 'May I ask what's prompting the move so soon after you bought this house?'

'It's a job change. There are some new opportunities for me in Norfolk. You can't beat a bit of variety in life anyway.'

'It's the spice of life, so they say.' Hotson pulled a pen out of inside jacket pocket so that he could make some notes.'

'I couldn't agree more. We would like to try and sell fairly quickly if we can.'

'Fair enough. I am going to take a quick look around. Obviously I won't need to measure up as we will have all that on file back at the office. Then we can discuss what price you want us to advertise the place for.'

'Oh, I've already decided on that one. I don't want to be greedy and, as I said, we would like a quick sale, so let's get it on at five hundred below what we paid.'

78

The following weekend the family made their way back down to Norfolk. Back past the drab industrial greyness at the start of their journey and then onwards though a landscape still bare from ravages of a hard winter, but striking nevertheless.

Graham and Suzanne were once again welcoming hosts.

'How wonderful to see you again Edward,' said Graham as his friend opened his car door after parking neatly next to the Rover on the large gravelled drive. 'Good journey?'

'Yes. We've done very well on time actually, despite Heath and his fifty mile per hour speed restriction.'

Graham laughed. 'Right well, let me help you with your bags and then you can come into the study and tell me all about your plans.'

Edward and Graham went into in the cosy little room overlooking the garden, whilst their wives and daughters made their way into the kitchen where they sat round a large pine kitchen table, drinking tea and eating some of Suzanne's delicious homemade sponge cake, and reacquainting themselves. Graham poured whisky into two tumblers and handed his friend one.

'So whereabouts are the houses you have arranged to see? It will be rather nice to have you living closer.'

There was genuine affection and respect between the two men and no matter which part of the county they settled in, Edward would only be a short drive away from his old companion.

'There are a couple of newish places we're going to tomorrow morning just south of the city. Then in the afternoon we've got the red brick cottage and the 1930's detached house I told you about on the telephone. It's a fairly full itinerary. If we like the look of any of them, I shall be asking for your valued opinion.'

'And I shall be pleased to give it Ed. Cheers!'

They chinked their whisky glasses together and Edward handed his friend the estate agents particulars of the properties he had shortlisted. Graham looked through them with interest and gave Edward his professional opinion on the merits of each. Being fairly familiar with the county he was able to supply some information about the advantages and disadvantages of the location of the properties.

'How easy do you think it will be to sell your house back home? Presumably you're going to need to find a buyer for that before you can buy down here?'

'It's already on the market. Board went up yesterday and the agent is fairly confident that he can find us a buyer soonish. Although, he would say that, wouldn't he?' Edward laughed. 'It is in one of the nicer areas of the town, so we have that on our side. The nice areas are outnumbered by the grotty areas and at the moment there's not much in the way of competition from other houses on the market. I think sellers are all sitting tight to see how things progress with this blasted three day week fiasco.'

Graham was amused at his friend's flawed logic, but said nothing as he knew it was founded in optimism, and that was a trait he had always admired in his friend. After all, what would be would be. He wanted Edward to be happy and, just a little bit selfishly, he wanted his friend to be in Norfolk and living closer to him. It would be wonderful to have a good male friend like Edward close by; they could share ideas, reminisce about their student days and go to the pub together.

Graham reached for the whisky bottle to top up their glasses without needing to ask if Edward wanted a refill. 'Oh, I've just remembered,' he said as he carefully poured a generous slug of the delicious amber liquid into Edward's tumbler. 'I spoke to Dennis on the 'phone a few days ago. Managed to track him down via his brother.'

'Really? That's great. How is the dear chap?'

'There have been developments with Dizzy. She's back on the scene apparently. All reconciled and she's seen the light. Things didn't work out with the object of her affection. Dennis has agreed to cut back on the hard stuff and so far all is well.'

'Good,' said Edward. 'That's good to know. Here's to Dennis.' Edward chinked his friend's whisky glass again and took a big long slug from his own.

79

The four houses on Edward's shortlist were viewed, as arranged, the following day. The two modern houses were ruled out due to their size and location. First call of the afternoon was to the empty and dilapidated Victorian cottage. It was situated at the end of a country lane in a quiet village. The large garden stretched to the side and rear of the house and beyond the boundary at the back were open fields and common land. The garden itself was overgrown but it did have a pretty brick outbuilding with a rusty corrugated iron roof and two handsome scots pine trees which were at the entrance to a little orchard. Edward liked the symmetry of the house. The front door with its decaying faded paint and crumbling portico above had sash windows equidistant on either side. There were three further sash windows above, all perfectly positioned over the features below them. The pantiles on the roof looked in reasonable order, Edward noted, but the chimney would need repointing. It was apparent that the back of the house was of a much earlier construction. The walls were made of brick and flint and the roofline was lower, angled down to a single storey at the very back. The cottage windows here were in no better condition than those at the front. They were old with flaking paint and the odd cracked pane of glass. Lizzie and Becky were amused by the separate outside brick toilet with its huge wooden seat and high level cistern, complete with rusty chain. The heavy and tatty wooden door of the privy was propped open with a brick and a pile of leaves had blown into the corner.

There was a fine drizzle falling and almost no breeze. Edward stood still in the garden and listened for a few seconds. No traffic noise, no distant sirens and no arguing neighbours. Just birdsong, the sound of his wife and children talking very quietly and the rhythmic 'plop, plop, plop' of rainwater falling from a broken iron gutter onto the metal dustbin below it.

'Why are you whispering?' Edward laughed. 'No one lives here!'

He unlocked the back door and they went inside. Lizzie thought the house might be haunted by the ghost of the old man who had lived here all his life until, according to the agent from where they had collected the key, he had died aged ninety four sometime the previous year. Becky was equally trepidatious, not because she was worried about ghosts, but because the house smelled very musty and huge cobwebs were hanging from the braded light cables and around the window shutters. Molly observed the old wallpaper peeling from the damp walls and the filthy threadbare rugs in each of the two front downstairs rooms.

'Shall we take a look upstairs now?' Edward asked after they had looked in each of the rooms on the ground floor.

The stairs creaked as they walked up to the half landing and then round the corner to the first floor. There were four large bedrooms, all with peeling wallpaper and dirty bakelite light switches like the rooms downstairs. The two back bedrooms had damp stains on the ceiling in the corners and there was no bathroom.

Molly and her daughters nervously assessed all that was obvious, but Edward's head was full of possibilities for improvement and opportunity to take on something that would give him a sense of fulfilment. By the time he had finished, this house would be evidence of his eminent capabilities. The floors would be dug up and replaced, the rising damp would be cured, the roof and gutters would be repaired, the walls would be re-plastered and those wonderful fireplaces and sash windows would be restored to their original glorious state. It was going to make a wonderful home.

80

Back in Humberside, Edward's plans soon all began to bear fruit. They found a buyer for their house and an offer was accepted on the dilapidated cottage in Norfolk. Molly was, on the one hand, alarmed at the speed of the progress and on the other relieved that she would soon be able to escape from her troublesome and persistent admirer. She was also concerned about the financial cost of another house move.

'What if you haven't found another job by the time we're due to move?' she dared to ask Edward one morning.

'Well, I'm sure I will, but in any event I've spoken to my mother about it and she's prepared to lend me a few hundred pounds which will keep us ticking over until something comes up. Her loan is also going to fund the cost of the caravan. And like we've said before, we will live in that while the house is being done up, then we can sell it again when we've finished with it and repay her. There's always a demand for these things. It won't be a problem.'

Molly wasn't sure that she wanted to be indebted to her mother-in-law in this way again, but it seemed Edward had it all arranged. In any case, her husband had now handed in his resignation at the Council so there was no going back.

81

29th March 1974 was the date set for the move. A year and thirteen days had passed since Hammonds Removals had pulled up on the drive of 186 Winchester Road. It had been twelve months of rejection, grief, disappointment, and sometimes fear. Admittedly, punctuated here and there by odd moments of joy spent in the company of old and new friends, but in the main it had been a year that no member of the Greenacre family wished to repeat.

Edward backed the car out of the garage and parked it on the road outside so that the removal van would have easy access to the driveway. It was due to arrive very soon.

Molly was sweeping the step at the front door and looked over to her husband as he locked the car door. She noticed a huge scrape running along the rear wing of the car and along both doors too.

'Whatever's happened to the side of the car?' asked Molly as Edward walked back up to the house.

'Someone drove into it on the staff car park yesterday. Well, that or they have deliberately damaged it. Who knows? They didn't report it so I will never find out.'

'Oh Ed. That's awful.'

'I can't worry about it now. It will get fixed when we're the other end and it probably looks worse than it really is. It's just one more thing for us to add to the long list of reasons why we're justified in moving from here. It's the kind of thing some people do round here it seems. Come on. Don't worry. Put that broom down and let's go and pack the last few bits and pieces so that we're ready for the van. They'll be here any minute. And the sooner we're away from here, the better.'

Within two hours the van had arrived, been loaded up and was now pulling out of the drive to start its 120 mile journey southward.

Molly and the girls had a final check round the house and got into the car. Edward put the last of the small items into the boot.

'Everyone alright?' he enquired as he sat in his seat, closed his car door and started the engine.

'Yes. We're alright,' replied Molly, looking round at her daughters to ensure they were settled.

'Let's go then.'

Edward drove to the end of the close and turned right into the main road. He looked down at the mileometer which read 47,884 miles and calculated that it would be showing 48,000 when they reached their destination. A destination which promised contentment and fulfilment. No longer would he be constrained by bureaucracy or the repercussions of unpleasant office relations. He would be free to build a better future for himself and his family and it would be on his terms. The Greenacres were on the cusp of becoming prosperous and successful and he was going to revel in the adulation and admiration that would be rightfully his, when, in a very short space of time, he had achieved these ambitions.

'Onwards to better things,' said Edward and turned briefly to smile at Molly.

Molly smiled back.

'Better things,' she repeated.

82

Mid spring had arrived and with it all the glorious abundance of plant, animal and insect life which was so welcome after months of lifelessness, cold weather and drab skies. Today was the perfect spring day. The sunshine was lighting up the fresh green leaves in the trees and dappled light was falling on to verdant grass. Tiny wisps of high cloud were scuttling across the blue sky. In the distance a cockerel was crowing and enthusiastic voices could be heard coming from the cricket pitch on the village green.

'Ed. I've got something I need to talk to you about.' Molly and Edward were sitting in the garden of their new home. The builders had been working inside all week, knocking old plaster off the walls, pulling up the floors and ripping out antiquated plumbing, but today was Saturday so there was a break from the dust and noise. The garden was large enough for the garden table and chairs to be situated well away from the builders' materials and tools which they had left messily strewn around the back door.

'Oh. That sounds serious.'

'Well it is. Kind of.' Molly's voice intimated at calm concern for something.

'Come on then Molly. Spill the beans. What important information do you need to impart?' Ed looked at Molly as she poured tea into two china mugs. I don't look at her enough, he thought. Her she is. My wife. My Venus. With her beautiful features framed by that golden hair and her slender hands, adorned by the symbols of our love - a diamond ring and a gold band. She placed the teapot back on to the table, wrapped her hands around her mug and looked down into her tea.

'Look at me Molly. Tell me.'

'I'm not sure how to start. It's a big thing I need to tell you.' Molly looked up at her husband and felt nervous but relieved that she could now unburden herself from five years of secrecy. 'It's sort of about Mum.'

'Your mother? She's alright isn't she?'

'Yes, she's fine. But something happened to her a long time ago and it had consequences. That's what I need to tell you about.'

'Go on,' said Edward.

'Before she met my Dad, when Mum was only about nineteen, she was attacked by a man. Raped.'

'Oh no. How awful. Poor Phyllis. That's just so awful.' Ed leaned forward and held his head in his hands. 'I can't believe it. How on earth has she felt living with something like that for all these years?'

'Ed' said Molly, stretching across to her husband and touching his forearm tenderly. 'There's more. She became pregnant.'

Edward looked up at her, astonished by what he had just heard. 'Molly ... I'm so sorry. How terrible.'

Molly took a breath and continued. 'My Granny and Grandad sent her away to have the baby and he was unofficially adopted by a couple who lived on the other side of the city.'

'I can't believe this Molly. How long have you known this? Why didn't you tell me?'

'Shush. Listen. I couldn't. The baby, James, grew up with that couple and Mum went back home to live with Granny and Grandad like nothing had ever happened. To the outside world anyway. Then she met my Dad and never ever told him about James. She's had to live with that guilt all her life.'

'But why should she feel guilt? She was raped for God's sake.'

'She felt guilty because his adoptive parents didn't treat him well at all. He had an awful upbringing Ed. Really terrible. And Mum came to know that. But she couldn't just suddenly tell Dad about him. It was a really awful situation.'

'When did you find out? When did she tell you all this Molly?'

'She didn't tell me. She doesn't know that I know.'

'What? Well how did you find out then?' Edward was perplexed.

'James found out about the circumstances of his birth and traced my Mum. It was easy. They lived in the same city and it had been an unofficial adoption. He was about twenty at the time. Mum was distraught. Distraught because she hadn't seen him since he was three days old, distraught when he told her all about the maltreatment and also because she was so scared Dad would find out. She'd got me, Rose and Gordon by then and Dad's health was beginning to fail.'

'Oh Molly. This is so sad. I can't believe all this.'

'When James realised that he was going to be unable to have any kind of meaningful relationship with Mum he tried hard to let go and get on with his life. But of course he had found out about me, Rose and Gordon and then, five years ago, came to find me. That's how I discovered it all.'

Now aware of the profound impact this revelation must have had on Molly, he leaned towards her and took her hands in his. 'Molly, this is dreadful for you. How have you kept this secret? Why? Why have you not told me before?'

'Keeping the secret was awful, yes, but I couldn't be more pleased to have James in my life. He's a wonderful man, Ed. He's my brother.'

'But I still don't understand why you haven't told me before.'

'I couldn't ask you to face Dad with that knowledge. He never did know about James and if you had known I am sure you would have felt that you were betraying him. I didn't want you to have to feel like that. James felt exactly the same. He didn't want to be responsible for anyone else having to keep such a huge secret.'

Ed squeezed Molly hands, leaned further towards her and kissed her tenderly on her forehead. 'You're an angel Molly. I adore you.'

'Where is James now? I mean, where's he living? Is he still here in Norfolk?' Ed had so many questions that needed answering.

'He's just moved back here, Ed. From Eastwater.'

'Eastwater? Was that just a coincidence? How did he come to be there?

'We were living at Winchester Road when he first made contact with me. At that point in his life, Ed, he was suffering. He was sad. Very sad. His relationship with his adoptive parents had completely broken down and Mum wouldn't, or couldn't, re-unite with him. Rose and I were his only other close blood relatives and he came to me because, I suppose, he felt like he needed to 'belong' somewhere.'

'Does Rose know about him?'

'No.'

'Why not?'

'I didn't want her to know. Again, because that knowledge could have been damaging to her relationship with Dad. She was so close to him, Ed. She worshipped Dad.'

Edward leaned back in his garden chair and put his hands across his eyes. He was shocked and saddened in equal measure.

'Here's the strange thing though, Ed. The day James first made contact with me was the day of Gordon's funeral. It's like he'd found a sister and lost a brother in one fell swoop.'

'What?' Edward's hands fell back into his lap.

'I know. It's so SO strange. Like it was meant to be.'

'And similarly you'd lost one brother and found another.'

'That's exactly how I see it Ed. Exactly.' Tears began to well in Molly's eyes and she brushed them away with her hand.

'So how come James was in Eastwater?'

'After the initial contact I met up with him several times and he decided to move down from Norfolk to be near me. He called me 'his lifeline'. He saw it as a huge turning point in his life. It was a huge responsibility for me, Ed. I felt almost like I had to save him. When he suggested moving down, I told him we might not be there for ever. He knew it was a risk, but it was a chance he wanted to take. He found himself a job and relocated. We used to meet up in his lunch break or after work sometimes and we've got to know each other really well. Obviously, when we moved away to South Humberside he was left behind on his own. I've been so worried about him, Ed. I really have.'

'Oh God, Molly. You should have told me. You should have.'

'I'm sorry Ed.'

Edward leaned over and kissed her forehead for a second time. 'Don't apologise. You don't need to.'

'I can't believe all this Molly. It's a lot to take in.'

'I know.'

Molly fell silent and let Edward sit back in his chair for a minute or two to digest the news she had just broken to him.

'Tell me about James. What's he like?'

'He's tall. Got Mum's pale blue eyes. And kind, Ed. He is such a kind and thoughtful man. I want you to meet him.'

'Of course. We must arrange that. And soon.' Edward paused for a second or two.

'What about your Mum? Has she had any contact with him since he was twenty?'

'None. James was astute enough to realise it would have huge and damaging repercussions if he tried to establish a relationship with her. And Mum's a stoic. You know that. She just got on with things and turned her attention to caring for Dad and for me, Rose and Gordon.'

'Are you going to tell her all this?' asked Edward.

'I've been thinking about that. Turning it over and over in my mind. The decision I have come to is that I should now talk to her about it. It's been a while since Dad died. I don't think it would be in any way disrespectful to him. And you know what? Dad was a lovely, kind, accepting, generous family man. If he is looking down on us now I am sure he would want Mum to be reconnected with her son. What do you think, Ed? Do you think that's an overly sentimental or fanciful thought to have?'

'Not at all. It's going to require some sensitivity, but I agree with you that you should talk to her about it. If you come clean with your Mum first then you can take things from there. Let that sink in and see how it goes. But I can't imagine for one minute that she wouldn't want to see her own son again.'

'I hope not. I think for everyone's sake, it's the best way forward.'

Edward picked up the teapot to top up their mugs. 'I can't believe this Molly. Such a shock. Five years you've known and absolutely no-one else has found out. Not me, not your Mum, not Rose. No-one.'

'Well,' said Molly, pausing and talking a deep breath. 'There were two other people who knew.'

'Molly? I don't understand. Who?'

'Diana and Peter.'

'Who?'

'Diana and Peter. Judith's parents.'

'What? Why? How come? I mean, why would you have told them?'

'I had to. Forced into it unfortunately. I often used to meet James on the seafront at Eastwater. One day Peter was walking past the bench were we always met and saw us. Put two and two together and made five sadly.'

'You mean he thought you were having an affair?' asked Edward incredulously.

'Yes. And he was very unpleasant about it at first. Kept teasing me, winking at me, enquiring after my 'fancy man' any time I was round at Diana's and she was out of earshot. I told him it wasn't what he thought. But he kept on and on Ed. He was horrible.'

'What a vile man. God I wish I'd know he was treating you like that.' Edward suddenly felt distressed that he hadn't been able to protect his wife.

'It's alright Ed. Honestly. I put up with it for as long as I could and then I told Diana the truth so she could hopefully get Peter to be quiet. His taunting did diminish to some extent, but he never really did believe me. And then we moved away and I didn't have to face him anymore.'

'Well look Molly – we're going up to see your Mum tomorrow so let's just do this thing. No time like the present. Too many wasted years have gone by already. I'll drop you off and leave you alone with Phyllis for a while so you can talk to her. What do you think?'

'Thanks Ed. Thank you for being so understanding. Thank you for helping me, and for helping James.'

83

Molly walked from the car which Edward had parked in the harbour car park and walked a short distance to an empty wooden bench by the wall which faced the water's edge. The tide was retreating and as it did so it revealed smooth, shiny ribbons of muddy sand on which various noisy seabirds were landing to peck about for their supper. There were several boats moored in the harbour, their lines chinking against the masts in the salty springtime breeze. In the distance an elderly couple stood silently against the metal railings which encased the harbour wall, looking out across the mudflats towards the open sea. The late afternoon sunshine danced on the water and lit up the sides of the boats which in turn reflected a rippling image onto the shallow sea.

    Molly shivered slightly as she sat down on the bench and pulled her coat over her knees. Her mood was a mixture of excitement and trepidation. She looked over towards the elderly couple and wondered what their history might be. Their stance suggested contentment. For a minute, Molly imagined that this might be an all-encompassing contentment with their present surroundings, with each other, with their past and the here and now. And yet Molly knew no-one's life could be a perfect thread of happy events, environments and relationships, no matter how hard some people would strive to portray such an image. That human thread was knotted and tangled in places and perhaps frayed and worn between the nice, smooth straight bits. Molly was grateful for her life thus far. Her own story had been a gently undulating path, punctuated every now and then with unbridled happiness and fortunately, less often, with short term distress, which she had always managed to overcome. The last five years had been testing to say the least.

'Molly.' A familiar voice came from behind her. Molly stood up and turned around to face James, who walked around the bench and immediately threw his arms around her in a wonderful embrace.

'It's so good to see you. I have missed you so much.' said James as he released her from his hold.

'I've missed you too.' Molly was beaming and took hold of James's hands and squeezed them tightly. 'Oh my, James. I am so relieved to see you. And look at you! You look so well and happy. Are you happy?'

'I'm happy Molly. I've never felt so happy in fact'.

'Are you ready to meet Edward?' asked Molly.

'I'm ready. And look Molly, I am so sorry that you had to keep me as a secret from him. I know it's been really difficult for you.'

'You don't need worry about it now. Water under the bridge,' replied Molly, smiling again and letting go of his hands. 'I have explained to him why I couldn't tell him any earlier. Like we discussed and agreed, it wouldn't have been fair on him to ask him to keep a secret like that. He had a lovely mutually respectful relationship with my Dad. That might have been skewed if he'd known about you and I am so sorry about that. So sorry. You are absolutely nothing to be ashamed of, James. I'm proud of you and so happy to call you my brother. Come on. Ed's over there in the car. Come and meet him then we'll go and get a cup of tea somewhere.'

84

Edward parked the car on the street at the front of the house. The house where something profound was about to occur. The house that had witnessed so much over the years. Happiness and sadness, peacetime and war, growth and decay, prosperity and hardship.

'How are you feeling James?' asked Molly, looking over her shoulder to the back seat where her half-brother was sitting.

'I'm fine. Really. Just a bit nervous.'

'You've nothing to be nervous of. It's all going to be alright. Mum and I have spoken at length and she is so happy that you have come to meet her again. I promise, it's all going to be alright. Come on, let's go inside.'

Edward, Molly and James got out of the car and walked round to the back door.

'Mum,' called Molly as she pushed open the door and they all went inside. The kitchen was warm and smelled of baking. Two halves of a victoria sponge cake were cooling on wire racks on the kitchen table. 'We're here Mum.'

Phyllis walked through from the front room. In front of her she saw Edward, her eldest daughter and James. A tall, handsome, fully grown man. Smiling at her.

'Hello Phyllis.'

Phyllis stretched out both hands towards him and he took them in his.

'It's Mum. Call me Mum.'

'Hello Mum.'

'Welcome home son.'

Printed in Poland
by Amazon Fulfillment
Poland Sp. z o.o., Wrocław